A FOREST OF VANITY AND VALOUR

THE LEVANTHRIA SERIES

A.P. BESWICK

To my awesome backers who have enabled me to create this book.

Laban P. Crook, Jonathan Cole, James Molnar, Brodie Selzer, Harley Hannon, Mumty, Carl Farber, Billy Coghill, Andromeda Taylor-Wallace, Jacon P. Winn, Bryant Diaz, De Winter Tim, Christian Holt, Julia A, Mattia Gualco, Dylan Bardon, Denis S. Hakes, Sharina Brock, Steph, Max Lindberg, Matt Snellgrove, Sy Hughes, and Rob Radcliffe.

You are all legends in my eyes, thank you.

To my beta readers Madelief, Debbie, Chris and Quinn. Thank you, your feedback and critique has helped shape this story.

TO THE MERRY MEN.....AND WOMEN

Seth (The Little) Alexander

Joshua (The Scarlett) Gray

Daniel (The Friar) Dorman

Robin (The Hood) Hill

Levanthria
...terian Plains
Uster
...ntar
Yugo's Tears
N
...Rivah
Voraz
Zakron Keep

BOOK ONE OF
THE LEVANTHRIA SERIES

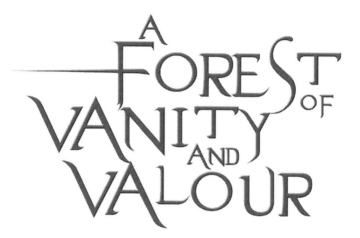

A FOREST OF VANITY AND VALOUR

I

VIREO

"Magic is an unnatural, unstable force. Even those with the greatest resilience succumb to the addiction."

-Hector Doren, scholar, 104 KR

I look up at the moon, its reflective light casting a crescent shadow over the ginnel where I hide. A foul stench is in the air, bad enough that with every breath I take, I taste the muck that lines these wretched streets. I let out a sigh of frustration. We are crouched, hiding in the slums, and my legs grow increasingly numb.

"Vireo." Lek hisses my name under his breath, trying not to draw attention to us. His colossal frame casts a shadow large enough for Gillam and me to hide under. His full brown beard engulfs his face, giving him the appearance of a wild man, but his armour tells a different story. His family crest – a bear with two axes above it, framed within the emblem of a shield – indicates his privileged background. It is a badge that Lek has worn with pride his

1

entire life. The man is a beast on the battlefield, someone I certainly would not like to be on the wrong side of.

"I am tired of waiting," I whisper, an air of impatience apparent in my voice. "Must we continue to hide in this hole any longer?"

"If we are to claim what is owed to us, then yes. We will wait here as long as necessary, Vireo." I glance to my left where Gillam crouches beside me. Her slender physique equips her with an unrivalled agility. Her long blonde hair is slicked back into a tight ponytail, and her amber eyes catch the light from the moon like a cat in the dark.

"We are not all built for the shadows like you, Gillam," I snipe at her, growing ever more frustrated. The repugnant smell makes me want to retch.

"The shadows are the safest place to hide." Gillam smiles as her well-spoken words roll off her tongue.

I look out across the street at the small building we have surveyed for the last three hours. Its windows are broken and boarded, and the walls are cracked with age. I wonder how anyone could bear to live in the derelict and overcrowded houses that line these streets. An odd flicker of light catches my attention from the moth-eaten curtains hanging in the windows where the poorest families live. A fair-haired, barefoot girl runs past me, gripping what looks like bread in her hands. Her footsteps splash the greying mud on my clothes.

"Blasted!" My voice rises. "This is ridiculous."

"Calm down, Vireo." Gillam smiles at my misfortune, which angers me further.

"I am not in the mood for your patronizing words, Gillam." I could happily strike her, my patience now at breaking point.

"Look." Lek draws our attention to movement ahead of us.

A hooded figure strolls to the door we have been watching. He hurriedly unlocks it, then gives one last nervous look around before disappearing into the darkness inside.

"Told you it would be worth the wait," Gillam sneers at me.

All we need to do now is reclaim what is ours. I pull my hood over my head as we make our way across the road, the mud squelching under my feet. I cannot wait to be home.

2

VÍREO

With a thud, Lek slams his club-like fist into the door three times with thunderous force. It is a wonder that the door does not crumble under his strength. We wait a moment for a response, but given how elusive our target has been, I am not surprised when the knock goes unanswered.

I let out a sigh, knowing where this is headed. I just wanted a quick and easy collect tonight and now I have wasted my evening hiding in shadows, crouched in this cesspit. But it is unavoidable; we must collect what is owed to Jareb, to the crown.

Lek hammers on the door once more. An old man walks by, pushing his cart down the street behind us.

"Little pig, little pig, let us come in," Gillam teases as she places her face to a hole in the door. "Or we will huff."

"Blasted." Lek cuts in and steps forward, taking a large lunge with his boot. He throws his leg in a frustrated kick, smashing the rotten door to pieces.

The hooded figure is instantly upon us. He swings a wooden batten at Lek's head, and Lek is barely able to move out of the way. Enraged, Lek picks up the man and throws him backwards, slamming him through some old shelves. The mites have already eaten through the wood, but the spectacle makes Lek appear even more powerful. The man lets out a large groan as he climbs back to his feet, his face hidden by the darkness of the room. Lek and Gillam step forward.

"Let's not make this more difficult than it needs to be." I speak with every intent of this ending quickly, but the man ignores my offer to do things the easy way.

He pulls his hand behind him and mutters under his breath.

My eyes widen as I see an unnatural glow behind his back. "He's a mage!" But the warning is too late.

The mage swings his hand in front of him and sends a jolt of power straight into Lek's chest, his chain mail acting as a conduit for the lightning. The house shakes as he hits the floor and begins convulsing. For a moment, I wonder if he will fall through the floor from the impact or if this ramshackle house will fall on top of us. I dive behind a table for cover as Gillam lunges for the mage. The mage is onto her, though, and mutters more words. She bounces off him as though an invisible wall is in the way.

Gillam climbs back to her feet, staring at the mage with fascination as I rise from behind the table and smile at him.

"You are a rarity," I call over. "Let us take what you owe, and we will leave you in peace."

"What I owe?!" His anger is apparent. "I have nothing left. Your people have taken everything away from me. EVERYTHING."

"We would fetch quite the coin for handing you over to Jareb," Gillam teases as she dusts down her clothes.

"That is not going to happen," I bark back. I am all for

collecting coin, but I draw the line at kidnap and trafficking. A mage that owes money would live out the rest of his life in servitude to the crown. The sheer fact he has displayed his magic towards us shows how desperate he must be. "Listen, you clearly have magic within you. I think those spells will have taken quite the energy from you. Just give us what is owed, anything of value, and we will leave."

My words fall on deaf ears as the mage's hand lights up once more. He releases a flashing light at Gillam, sending her soaring across the room and out of the broken front door. At least the mud makes a soft landing for her. The mage spins with his focus solely on me now. He is moving slower than before, and I can see he is fatigued. He draws his hand back and I grab my moment – I lunge forward, taking the mage off guard as I grab the scruff of his neck and slam him against the wall. My forearm presses tightly against his chest as I clasp my left hand over his mouth.

"One more spell from you and I will remove your tongue," I warn with gritted teeth. The mage continues to struggle against me, but I am far more powerful than he is. I strike him around the side of the head and his body becomes limp as he slips into unconsciousness.

3

JAREB

"*Following his daughter's assassination at the hand of a maid wielding magic, King Graden IV banished the practice throughout Levanthria. Overnight mages, witches, seers, and healers were outlawed and hunted down like animals. Those that were not slaughtered were branded and forced into a life of slavery.*"

-*Fivera Dorian, member of the Queen's guard, 131 KR*

I stand by the window in my bedroom, the fire behind me providing me warmth and comfort within the walls of the castle. In the king's absence, the weight of the land falls on my shoulders, and I just pray that I am doing him proud.

"Are you ok, dear?" Allana's arms wrap around me from behind and I cover her hands with mine. Together, we gaze out the window at the city beyond the castle walls. "Come back to bed."

"I can't rest." I turn to face her and place my hands on the sides of her arms. Her long dark hair falls to the small of her back. Her skin is pale, her eyes like ice. Her unnatural beauty still takes my breath away every time I see her. "I want the war to be over so things can go back to normal."

"We all do," she reassures me. "Someone has to hold the castle in the king's absence. Someone has to ensure the king and his soldiers continue to have supplies while they are at war." She understands the need for me to enforce the decisions I've made, but I can't help but wonder if she truly understands the burden my situation places on me.

I want to help the people and see this once prosperous land of Levanthria flourish again. "I can't bear to see such a large portion of the population living in poverty as they are now, but if we are to end this war, we must continue to collect money and supplies from them." My words are true, but I worry the people are growing tired with the taxes they must pay in order to fund the king's latest war.

"It is not your decision to do this, my love." Allana's voice is soft and hypnotic, as though singing me a lullaby, instantly reassuring me.

"It is a decision that I have to enforce though, Allana. One that makes people from across the land dislike me." I turn away from Allana and look out once more over the darkness of the city. I can feel my frustration building and I take in a large breath to calm myself. Allana's soft grip wraps around me once more as she attempts to settle me.

"My love, you are a good man."

"The people do not agree with you on that, though. Look at the way so many are suffering in these times. I need to find a way to make it easier for them. Their conditions are no fault of their own." I speak my words from my heart. There is no greater pain than having to follow actions that go against every fibre in one's being. If we are going to win this war, I must stay strong, for the people of the kingdom and for the king.

The one thing keeping me from losing my sanity is Allana. I do not know what I would do without her. It is as if the gods sent her to me as a gift to aid me with my struggles. Her years are much fewer than the forty-five that I have walked this earth, and I often wondered what she sees in an aging aid to the king. I am long past my physical prime, and I am greying. My face now shows how weary I have become, and my brow is lined where it was not previously.

"We must win this war, Allana. I need to help our people more. Maybe then I will sleep."

4

VIREO

The mage seems to realise that struggling is pointless. Lek and Gillam grasp his arms, taking a tight hold to prevent him from escaping.

"You need to pay what is owed," I remind the mage.

"I have already told you, you fool. I have nothing." There is a resilience in the mage that I admire. However, the night is getting late, and I am growing tired of this. I want to be at home in the warmth, away from this filth. Instead, we must continue to press for the coin that Jareb has requested.

I nod at Lek. He strikes the mage in the stomach, who lets out a large gasp, instantly winded. I crouch down to bring myself level with him. The dampness in the air leaves a bitter taste in the back of my mouth. "Everyone has to pay."

"For a war none of us wanted?!" the mage spits back at me. "Our people are suffering, yet you live in your manor."

"I have paid my dues." The mage's words irk me. "For collecting coin for Jareb, he allows me to keep my manor."

"You're just as bad as Jareb, then, if you're happy to live in luxury at our expense."

My temper flares and I grab the mage by the scruff of his cloak and bring his face close to mine. Close enough to smell the stench of his stagnant breath in my face. "You are lying. You must have some coin hidden away somewhere."

"I gave it to Jordell." The mage avoids my eyes. I know I am getting to him. "He helps feed the poorest. I gave him my coin to help provide food for those that need it."

"Well, that was stupid," Gillam says. "Vireo, what shall we do with him?"

"What we do with anyone that does not pay what they owe to the crown." I turn from the mage and saunter toward the shattered front door. I feel my clothes are now ruined by the stench in the air that clings to my every fibre.

Lek and Gillam begin beating mage, ferociously knocking him to the floor where they continue to kick and punch him. He whimpers, unable to fight back.

"Like I said before, Vireo, we would fetch some coin for ourselves if we turn in a mage," Gillam presses us as she stands over the barely conscious man, his face bloodied and bruised.

"And I told you no." I raise my voice, annoyed at having to repeat myself. "We do not traffic, and we don't promote slavery."

I see the vein in Gillam's head throb with displeasure, but I know she will listen. We have been through a lot together we served our time on the front lines of the war in Ethua. "A beating is enough. Others will learn from this example."

Lek scoops the mage up from the floor with one hand and draws his tightly clenched fist back, ready to strike one last blow.

The mage is clearly disorientated but as I make my way to the door to leave, he speaks quietly, broken. "No more, please," he splutters, a bloody trail leaving his nose, his lips swollen. "In the back, there is a door under the rug."

The mage has been a fool for not telling us this sooner. All this could have been easily avoided if he had only listened to me at the start. I nod towards Lek, who releases the mage, dropping him to the floor.

The floorboards creak under my weight as I make my way to the back of the room and push open the door. It surprises me that it doesn't fall from its hinges. I grab hold of a mite-ridden bed frame and slide it to the side. The scratching noise sends a shiver down my spine, and I am pleased to see the mage has been true to his word. In front of me, there is a small hatch with a little metal handle, covered in a heavy layer of dust. I reach down to pull the door open, excited to see what valuables lie in wait.

I am intrigued by what I see inside. Not money or treasures, but a leather-bound book. It has intricate stitching on the outer edge, with words and symbols that have no meaning to me etched into the front. I know instantly that the book has value, and it takes my breath away. Jareb will be happy.

For it is not just any book. It is the rarest of finds.

It is a book of spells.

5
VIREO

"And so the bloodiest day in Levanthria's rich history became known as the Benighted Thaumaturgist. A day that darkness engulfed those with the gift of magic. Thousands murdered for the actions of one. Those that were lucky enough to survive went into hiding."
    -Hansen Willem, A History of Levanthria, 251 KR

When we arrive back at my manor, our stench fills the entranceway to a point where even my working staff look repulsed. The maid gags as she takes my cloak away to be washed.

"Take these two stinking dogs to the guest-rooms and run them baths. I cannot bear to be around them any longer."

The staff lead Gillam and Lek off onto the far side of the manor, where I know they will be happy with the comfort of warm baths and fresh clothes while their armour is cleaned for them.

I follow the hallway that leads to my chambers. The walls

are filled with the portraits of my father, grandfather, and great grandfathers, stretching back the last four hundred years. I glance at my father's portrait, which hangs closest to my chambers. His dark eyes observe me whenever I walk past, as if he is watching me from the afterlife. His eyes are the only recognizable trait that I inherited from him; luckily, I take after my mother. It has been seven years since they both passed, and seven years since I inherited this manor and all their coin.

I enter my chambers. My large bed sits in the centre, which has gilded bed posts that reach high towards the ceiling, a sheer drape surrounding them. If I wasn't so filthy, I could happily dive in and go to sleep.

Ornate decorations fill the sides of the room. A deer head and a bear head hang off the wall – trophies of beasts I had taken down while hunting in previous years. In front of the bed is a large white rug made from the hide of a polar bear, an exotic gift given to me on my twenty-second birthday by my parents. It is one of the last things they gifted me before their death at the hands of bandits. Had it not been for the driver who had taken a shortcut on route to Eltera, my parents would still be here.

In the far side of my chamber, my maids have already prepared my copper bath in anticipation of my arrival. I cannot wait to get out of these stinking clothes. I'll have to remember to tell the maids not to bother washing them; they should throw them out, or better yet, burn them.

After, I make my way to the great hall where I devour a roast chicken prepared by the kitchen staff. The hall serves as the centrepiece of the manor where my wealth is on full display. The large oak table in the middle of the room is where I find myself sitting with Gillam and Lek, ploughing through our midnight feast with the etiquette of savages.

Even more trophies of animals and unique pieces of artwork decorate the walls. All round the outer edges are different vases and ornaments from across the land that my mother had collected in her time.

"You eat like an animal." Gillam's attention focuses on Lek, whose bear-like hand is wrapped around a chicken leg. The juices pour down his large beard, and Gillam looks visibly repulsed.

"This food is good, and well-earned after today," Lek fires back, unfazed.

He may give the appearance of a wild man in armour with mannerisms that don't suit his nobility, but Lek is easily the most loyal man I have ever met. He has been by my side throughout my life and saved it countless times, a debt I can never repay other than ensuring that he never goes without. I love the man like a brother, and he also served by my side in the war at Ethua with Gillam.

"Finish your food, we have an early start tomorrow." Perhaps Jareb will be impressed with the spell book we found and provide us with some extra provisions as a thank you.

Lek wipes his mouth with the arm of his sleeve, then picks up his tankard of ale and guzzles it down before releasing an enormous belch and standing up. I see him look across at the portrait of my parents with me standing in front of them as a child, and I wonder what he is thinking.

"We live like bachelors, and I enjoy the life we live, but do you ever think we are getting to an age where we should settle down and produce heirs?" His deep voice echoes in the hall.

Gillam and I burst into laughter.

"That's enough ale for you, my friend." Gillam removes the tankard from Lek's hand, who looks most aggrieved.

I continue to gather myself from my laughter at Lek's deep thought process. "Why would I want to tie myself down to one woman when I can have as many as I would like?"

Gillam continues to chuckle. "We can barely look after ourselves, let alone other people. Can you imagine any of us with a child to care for, or a wife for that matter?"

Lek continues to look up at the painting, deep in thought.

"Your affection for women is your biggest weakness, Vireo. One day it is going to get us into trouble." He snatches his tankard back from Gillam and downs the rest of his ale before we all make our separate ways to our chambers for well-earned rest.

All I can think about is what Jareb's face will look like when he sees the spell book that we found.

That, and a certain dark-haired beauty who I can't wait to see again.

6

JAREB

The birds wake me as soon as they sing at the crack of dawn, and I know I will be unable to get back to sleep. As the sun rises, the light enters my chamber and I roll onto my side to observe Allana sleeping peacefully next to me. What does she dream about? I cannot remember the last time I had a peaceful dream. My decisions haunt me at night, often resulting in restless nightmares.

Not wanting to disturb Allana, I rise from bed and put on my robe before heading out onto the balcony to get some fresh air. It is at this point in the morning when the kingdom most resembles its former glory. There is a calmness and peace in the streets as the night's shadows disappear in exchange for the hustle and bustle of the day.

However short-lived this calmness is, I like to take it all in; it gives me hope that one day, we will return to our old ways.

In the courtyard, my soldiers march to change over the guard at the walls and main gate. Their dark armour catches the sun, and the reflection reveals the crest of the crown: a lion and a dragon facing each other, their claws drawn and ready for battle. Down to my right, some children help the cooks unload supplies into the storerooms.

It reminds me that today is a day full of meetings about taxes and collections from the city. The day that I hate more than any other. All the local nobility – or, as I prefer to call them, collectors – will try to grease me up by presenting whatever money they scavenged from the previous seven days. I will have to sit and appear grateful as the collectors peacock around, pretending they have worked extremely hard, when in fact all they have done is take coin from vulnerable people. Today will be a day where I have to bite down on my frustrations and pretend that the collectors have done well for the crown and king, even when I despise every one of them. Each of them stands for everything I have grown to hate about the king's foolish war. Greed, gluttony, vanity. Children starve and dress themselves in rags, while collectors sit in their large homes, exceeding their share of rations, wearing clothes that are made from the finest silk. No wonder the people of the city hate us all. I hate them just as much, but not as much as I hate myself for what I must do.

I grip the railing so tightly that my knuckles grow white. I gather myself and walk to my wardrobe, slowly opening it to reveal my clothes inside. Another wave of frustration fills me. Why must I have to wear such pompous, grandiose clothing to these meetings when the sheer amount of fabric on them could probably make sheets for those on the streets to keep warm? I pull out the red robe and dress myself quietly, not wanting to wake Allana. Her gentle breathing brings me the last of the peace I will find for the rest of the day. Then I sneak out of the room.

7

VIREO

"The Forest of Opiya is shrouded in dark magic. There are many creatures and beasts that reside in there. It is said that the god's themselves use it as a twisted playground for their experiments."

Freya Knach, Tales of Levanthria 142 KR

Early the next morning, I wait at the entrance door to the manor for Gillam and Lek to drag themselves out of bed. We plan to hunt before we head to the castle to see Jareb. Neither of them are as keen on hunting as I am, but I find nothing is better than escaping the city walls and hunting near the Forest of Opiya. That is where all the best game is, and the unnatural creatures that live within the forest ensure that no men stray near it, which means we have it to ourselves. I think Lek, Gillam, and I are the only ones stupid enough to hunt there. The bigger the risk, the better the reward. Besides, it's been over a month since we've gone out, and I'm feeling antsy.

Heavy footsteps sound as Lek and Gillam finally appear

from around the corner. Lek looks the freshest out of the three of us, and Gillam looks as though she hit the ale hard last night, her normally tightly-tied hair hanging loose and ruffled.

"You're late." I dislike being kept waiting.

Lek does not have a care about this. "And?" He shrugs it off. He knows he is twice my size and could crush me like an ant if he so wished.

Gillam doesn't appear fazed, either. In fact, she looks like she is about to be sick. "I don't feel so clever."

"Don't even think about vomiting on my floor. You can save that for outside. Like the dog you are," I tease her.

Lek gives Gillam a thunderous slap on the back "You should learn to hold your ale."

"I should learn not to go toe to toe with you." Gillam puffs out her cheeks to hold back another wave of nausea.

A short ride later with my cart and horses, we arrive just north of Askela near the edge of the Forest of Opiya, its large pointed pine trees standing tall on the far side of the field.

"Blasts, Vireo, do not get too close," Lek curses at me as I stop the horses and we come to an abrupt stop.

"Don't tell me you're afraid, Lek? The gods built you like a bear. What manner of creature could harm you?"

"Between an ice bear, hipporhine, and horned wolves, you know full well that it doesn't matter what my size is in there. I am a sitting duck in the forest, like anyone else." Lek's voice gets higher as he speaks, much to Gillam's and my amusement.

Truthfully, I have no intention of going any closer than we need to. Lek is right; no one in their right mind would enter the forest. But there is plenty of hunting to be done on its outskirts. Wild deer graze the fresh green grass, and they do not stray into the forest for the same reasons that we keep away.

"What if the beasties come out of the forest. What then?" Gillam prompts Lek further as she climbs out of the cart.

"They can't. The spell makes sure of that," Lek says seriously, not realising that Gillam is only teasing. We all know about the enchantment supposedly placed over the forest a millennia ago – one that trapped strange creatures within, preventing them from leaving. Even so, strange stories arise from time to time about people going missing from nearby villages, or strange beasts wandering in the night.

"Can we focus on the task at hand, please?" I hop down and open the back of the cart. I pull a gold-edged case towards me, its top decorated with an ornate, intricate pattern. Within it lies my prized bow, made from the wood from a great oak tree. Its polished look and carvings lend to its extreme beauty. It is an heirloom that has been in my family for as long as anyone can remember, and my father trained me on it vigorously. I am a dead shot with a bow and an arrow – the best in all Levanthria. No one is as proficient with a bow as I am.

When I grip the handle tightly, I feel a sense of empowerment. Like I can never miss my target. I raise the bow and draw it back to test its strength. It still feels perfect to the touch. I fire some practice shots before placing my quiver over my shoulder and setting off into the tall grass.

"You two stand watch while I go in," I command. The last thing I want is for any looters to catch us off guard and try to rob me. Lek and Gillam follow close behind as I wade into the grass.

The noise from the world disappears the second I enter the overgrown meadow. All I can hear is the rustling from behind me as Lek attempts to keep up. The man is about as subtle as a brick.

I raise my clenched fist into the air to show them to stop. If Lek carries on the way he is, he will scare off any wildlife in a five-mile radius. The pair of them stop straight away and I pause, taking in the still air around me, breathing in the soft scent of the grass. Then I see it.

The deer is grazing on its own without a care in the world. I nock an arrow and inhale a deep breath as I draw the string back. I'm ready to make the shot when there is a loud crunch behind me.

"Blast." I curse as the deer looks up and bolts. "You are an oaf," I hiss behind me at Lek. I aim my bow into the air, estimating the deer's flight path. Then I release my arrow into the sky. A few seconds later, there is squeal and a thud as the deer hits the floor.

"Perfect shot, as usual." Lek tries to sound nonchalant, but his eyes are wide with awe.

"Nearly lost it because of you," Gillam points out. "You can carry it back for that."

Lek sets off farther into the grass and returns a few minutes later with the deer's carcass draped over his shoulders like a prized fur scarf a lady might wear. Except this one is covered in blood and impaled with an arrow.

"Dinner will be nice tonight!" A huge grin fights through his matted beard.

There is a rustle to our right and I am instantly drawn to a yelping noise. It sounds like a creature in pain.

"What the blazes is that?" Lek is quick to draw his axe.

The grass is long here, making it difficult to see. I reach forward to pull the grass to the side and I am shocked at what lies there.

The creature resembles a wolf but is much larger, its fur

thick and black like oil. Horns protrude from its head, forming dangerous spikes. It thrashes around, unable to move because of a snare wrapped around its leg.

"It's a wolfaire," I breathe.

"A wolfaire outside of the forest?" Gillam is puzzled and rightfully so; wolfaires rarely travel so far from their home.

"Perhaps it was stalking our deer," I suggest.

"Perhaps it was stalking us!" Lek spits. "I say we kill it where it lies."

As if it understands Lek's words, the wolfaire bares its pointed teeth and growls, hackles rising.

"No." I do not know why, but I feel we must help this creature. Maybe it is the sadness that I can see in its eyes. Has this wolfaire given up, resigning itself to its fate?

"You're mad," Lek protests, but I have made up my mind. Raising my hands, I lean towards the creature slowly.

"There, there, boy. I'm not going to hurt you." I tentatively reach for the wire snare wrapped around the creature's leg. He continues to growl at me, but he does not strike out. I remove the thin wire, revealing a gash in the wolfaire's leg.

The beast is now freed. I stand and stare at it, uneasy, and unsure of what it will do next. The growl turns into a low rumble in its throat. I take a step back. Then, it lets out a deafening howl and breaks into a run. It disappears into the grass, leaving us alone with our kill.

"That was a little close for comfort," Gillam chuckles.

I breathe a sigh of relief. "Let's get back with our dinner before the wolfaire changes his mind."

"Vireo, you are a fucking madman," Lek scolds me, but I ignore him. I know I have done the right thing in releasing the creature.

But it is nearly midmorning, and we must return to the manor so that we can prepare our week's spoils for Jareb.

On our way into Askela, I ponder our strange encounter with the wolfaire. Why was such a creature lingering outside the forest? How did it get past the enchantment?

But as we near the castle, which stands stunningly atop the highest point of the city, images of Allana emerge in my mind, replacing all thoughts of the beast.

I hope she'll be there when we arrive to present our offerings – and the spell book – to Jareb.

The thought makes my heart race.

8

JAREB

It is only midmorning and I have just ended the first meeting of the day. Renard and his men have dropped off a decent amount of supplies and coin, and had their egos massaged for their 'hard work'. It annoys me that these nobles insist on being praised, like dogs whining for a belly rub. They keep the coin and supplies coming and, in return, they do not have to enlist and fight in the war. They are all cowards in my eyes.

"My lord, until next week." Renard bows. His balding head reflects the light of the sun from outside. His toothy smile is as fake as they come.

When they're gone, I let out an enormous sigh.

"My lord, there is a report from the king." The boy's voice echoes in the Great Hall where I sit, and I instantly feel intrigued, my heart rate rising. The king does not write often. Maybe this is the letter we have been waiting for, the one to declare that they have won the war. The boy approaches. He is unkempt in appearance, his olive skin and dark hair covered in dirt from the streets.

The boy passes me the letter, his hands trembling. I try

to give him a small smile to show that he needn't be nervous around me. I am not the king, after all, but his steward.

I pull the letter from his hand hastily, vibrating with anticipation. I break the king's seal and remove the parchment from within it.

Jareb,

The war is taking its toll on us all. My soldiers grow weary from the travelling and fighting, and our numbers have fallen. I'm afraid that the enemy has the upper hand. They have magic. I have always thought of mages as rare, but the Zarubians have many in their ranks. They have an elite battalion of them, led by a mage with power I have never seen or heard of. He has the ability to bring down fire on our soldiers from above.

I write you this letter as a desperate plea for more supplies. We need more weapons, food, and horses. You must therefore increase taxation immediately. I need you to send more troops to help aid with the war.

I know this is a delicate request, but if we are to win this war, we need more supplies and more soldiers.

I also ask that the extra coin you take from the people of Levanthria be used to research magic, so that we may be able to fight back. For this reason, I need every known mage conscripted to our military forces immediately.

Faithfully,
King Almerion

My hands shake, and I feel the weight I already carry has been replaced with lead. I can feel my breath hastening and my heart pounds against my chest. A sharp pain sears across my head and I fall into the chair behind me, feeling as if the Great Hall is going to swallow me.

"Are you ok, my lord?" The boy's meek voice snaps me back.

I pour myself a drink from the pitcher on the table beside me, throwing it down my throat as I try to steady myself. I wipe away a bead of sweat that has trailed down my face. "I'm fine, boy. You may leave. Please take some fruit with you for your troubles." The boy's face lights up and he grabs as many apples as he can carry from the bowl on the table.

When he is gone, I re-read the letter, half-hoping I'd misunderstood the king's words. The orders are right there before me. If I don't follow the king's instructions – if I don't raise taxes in attempt to squeeze even more from the people of Levanthria, who are already suffering enough – it is likely that we will lose the war and it will be a short time before the forces of the Zarubian empire swell our lands. If I do follow his instructions, I fear what that means for our citizens. We could very well have a riot on our hands.

And how the blazes am I supposed to go about hunting down mages? They aren't exactly known for parading their abilities around in the streets for all to see.

I pour myself another drink of water and sink into my chair. I was right when I woke up this morning. Today is a terrible day.

9
VIREO

"*Minotaurs, centaurs, and fauns are just a few of the creatures that exist beyond Levanthria. Half-man, half-beast. It is said that Loria, the goddess of torture, cursed man and woman for not bending to her will.*
"

-Hansen Willem, Creatures of the World 220 KR

Gillam pulls the reins on the horses to draw our cart to a stop in front of the wrought iron castle gates. The large stonework is impressive; each block of stone is bigger than Lek. I chuckle to myself at my bizarre thoughts.

Towers on either side of the castle reach high up into the sky. This castle's sheer size is stunning. Askela is the capital of Levanthria, after all, and its headquarters need to live up to expectations.

Two guards walk towards us, spears in hand, and their armour clinks in unison to their synchronized steps.

"State your business," one guard commands, the tone in his voice telling me he is not in the best of moods.

"Are you stupid?" Gillam spits at the guard. "We deliver to Jareb every week."

The guard grips his spear tightly. He looks as though he'd love nothing more than to impale Gillam on it.

"I must apologise for my friend," I cut in, hoping to mitigate the situation. "You see, she is horrendously hungover." It's never good to get into an altercation before lunch. "As Gillam has stated, we have business with Lord Jareb. I think it is in your best interest to not delay us any further."

The guard seems less than impressed with the pair of us, but he knows he must let us in, and it is irking him more than usual. The guards signal through the bars at the side of the gate and the chains loosen. The large entranceway drops before us like a bridge.

Gillam urges the horses forward and we set off through the gates in our cart which is heavily loaded down with supplies. Gillam blows a kiss at the guard, and his fellow soldier puts an arm across him as he makes to lunge toward her in retaliation.

"Honestly, between your womanizing and your ability to wind people up, I am amazed we can still walk this world in the manner which we do," Lek's voice booms at us. "How the pair of you have not got us killed before now is beyond me." I can't help but feel like I am being scolded by a teacher.

We dismount at the centre of the courtyard and unload the goods. Lek carries the sack of coins and I cradle the package that contains the mage's spell book, which is wrapped carefully in linen. I don't want to take any changes.

The noise from the courtyard evaporates when we step inside. We are greeted by the large stained-glass window depicting King Nespiah, the ruler who created this castle eight hundred years ago. The light shines through it, painting the floor in front of us with coloured reflections. I've been in the castle countless times, but the sheer beauty and workmanship of that stained-glass window never ceases to inspire me.

A servant navigates us through endless, winding hallways, our footsteps echoing off the stone. Flags and emblems from all over Levanthria decorate the walls on either side of us, boasting how large our kingdom is. The aroma of freshly baked bread wafts from down the corridor and almost knocks me off my feet. The infectious smell puts me a million miles away from the squalor and odious stench I was forced to endure the night before, and I am relieved that it is only a memory now.

The servant comes to a halt in front of the large wooden doorway to the Great Hall, and knocks briskly.

"Come in," a voice calls.

We make our way inside for our collection meeting with Jareb.

IO

JAREB

The door opens and in steps Vireo and his enforcers. I can think of nothing worse than having to sit through a meeting with his smug, rugged face staring back at me. Another dog wanting his belly rubbed for taking money from the poorest. I try to hide my resentment by taking a large gulp of water.

"Please sit down." I stretch my hand out toward the chairs in front of me. Flanked by his cronies, Vireo swaggers across the Great Hall, which makes me want to dive across the table and strike him. Of all the nobility in Askela and surrounding lands, Vireo is the one I dislike the most. A man who truly takes pleasure in taking things that do not belong to him.

Vireo and the woman shuffle into their chairs and make themselves comfortable, but the large, wild-looking man struggles to fit in the seat because of his sheer build. In the end, he decides simply to stand up behind his chair.

"I know things are increasingly difficult for the people of Askela," I begin, "but I am afraid things are going to get worse before they get better."

The woman places a large sack onto the table which, judging by the jingle within, is clearly filled with coins. She casts me a smug grin.

"You have exceeded expectations, Vireo." I almost choke on my words as I force them out.

"What can I say? We have a skill for these things," he responds, smirking.

My urge to jump across the table and strike him overcomes me once more, but I push it back down and swallow my pride.

He continues, "It is the least I can do to ensure that we support King Almerion in his war effort. Please accept this coin."

"The king will be most pleased. I have received a letter from the His Majesty today, however, with dire news." I relay the contents of the letter, watching Vireo's expression change.

"The king wants to research magic?" He says with confusion on his face. There is something else in his expression, too – it almost looks like triumph, though I cannot imagine why.

"How much would a mage fetch?" The woman cuts in. Vireo flashes a firm look in the woman's direction, which I do not quite understand the reason for.

"There will be no reward for mages," I tell them sternly. "They need to be encouraged to join the ranks and aid us in this effort. They will be hard enough to find without forcing them into actions that they do not wish to engage in. I want the extra coin to go towards the mages, making sure they have food and supplies to hone their skills and further research their magic, which will hopefully give us an advantage."

"But magic, it's not natural," the large brute interjects.

"It is a curse from the gods and not meant for this world. The crown of Levanthria condemns it."

He is right, of course. For hundreds of years, magic wielders have been shunned and slaughtered like cattle, ever since King Graden the IV's daughter was assassinated by a witch.

"Yes, my lord, of course." Vireo's face tells the opposite story of his words. He places a bag on the table and unfastens it. "Maybe this will help you get started."

He pulls out a leather book and my eyes instantly widen. Its gilded edge and complex symbols are unmistakable; it is a spell book. I rise and make my way around the table to delicately take the book into my hands. It is deceivingly heavy. I open it to reveal pages upon pages of words and symbols that have no meaning to me. There is a musty smell clinging to the weathered parchment.

"Vireo, I need you to find Jordell and bring him here at once." We both know that Jordell works from the Great Temple in the centre of Askela, helping those in need. "He may be able to help us." Although I know Jordell is no mage, he has a talent for making potions through alchemy, and may be able to read this spell book.

The door to the Great Hall opens, and my head snaps up to see who would dare interrupt the meeting. I am surprised to see that it is Allana. She wears a tight-fitting green gown and looks truly mesmerising.

"I believe my uncle has written to you? May I see the letter?" Allana walks over to my chair and I hand her the letter. She begins to read, her face dropping.

"This can't be." She clasps her hand across her mouth.

Her concern shows me the compassion she and I share for the people of Levanthria, yet another reason why I love her so much.

"We have a plan, Allana. Thanks to Vireo and his men, we may have found something which we can use to encourage the mages to help us, rather than enslaving them."

Allana's gaze grazes the book on the table. Then she looks at Vireo and smiles. She moves closer to him and places her hand on his shoulder.

"Well done, Vireo. I am sure the king will be most pleased." She slides her hand away and turns to me. "I will leave you boys to discuss your plan. My love, I presume you will fill me in on the details once you have finished your meeting?"

"Of course, my love." I watch her walk away. Her swaying slender frame hypnotises me like a snake charmer.

I return my attention to Vireo. "Find Jordell straight away. Tell him about this spell book. Tell him that the king needs his help." Vireo drags his gaze away from the departing figure of my wife, and I can't help but notice the faraway look in his eyes.

II
VIREO

"He hates us," says Gillam as we make our way to the Great Temple to find Jordell. I can't disagree with her; the look on Jareb's face whenever he sees me does not go unnoticed. He always makes a poor job of hiding his distaste.

Nonetheless, the timing with the spell book could not have been any better. I can't help but feel that once we have collected Jordell from the temple, our efforts will be heavily rewarded. I feel certain that we will have cause for celebration tonight, with fresh venison to feast on besides.

We drive our cart towards the city centre. The well-kept streets and houses make a stark contrast against the squalor of the slums we visited last night. But I can't help but notice that there are fewer market stalls than usual. Perhaps the increase in taxation has run them out of business, but I push such thoughts away. I'm a collector, not a charity worker.

"The man has no backbone," Lek grumbles. Up ahead, a group of children are play fighting with weapons fashioned out of wood. "I would never let a woman speak to me how his wife did. It was just damn disrespectful." He is sitting with his back to us, surveying the street behind our cart as we move. Lek is always ready for a surprise assault when we're on the road, even if it is in the middle of the city.

"She is King Almerion's niece, Lek, and you must show more respect," I remind him. Lek may be of noble blood, but could still find himself in murky waters should anyone overhear his contempt for Allana.

"Such gallantry, Vireo," Gillam says, flashing a knowing smile. "I don't suppose there could be any *other* reason why you're defending her?"

I stare at her. Who does she think she is, to speak to me in such a manner? I need to stand my ground with her. I keep my gazed fixed on Gillam until Lek bursts into laughter, breaking the tension.

As we pass the playing children, I notice that one boy has quite excellent form for his age. It is only a matter of time until they enlist him to fight in the war, with real swords and real enemies.

"This alchemist best be at the temple. I have no time for errands," Gillam says as we pass a fish stall where a man is busy at work, filleting his morning catch. I make note of the size of the fish: it looks like he is in for a good day's trading, which means if we call back later, we should be able to claim the correct taxation from him before he has time to tamper with his earnings.

Then I have an idea. "Heel!" I call out, bringing the cart to a sudden halt. Its wooden wheels skid through the dirt, sending a plume of dust into the crowd.

Lek bowls over backwards into the back of the cart. "Blazes, Vireo, is there any need?"

"One moment." I jump down and hold out a small bag of coins to the fish merchant. "Give fish to as many as this coin will permit." A hungry crowd gathers around us, murmuring words of approval.

"Thank you."

"You are so kind, sir."

"Blessings."

Voices of praise circulate, and it is a feeling that gives me a rush. I could get used to this.

"What on earth was that for?" Gillam scratches her head in bemusement when I climb back onto the cart.

"Keep the folk on side, I see?" Lek is quick to deduce my reasoning for my random act of kindness.

I can't help but smile. "Don't worry, Gillam, we will be back later to collect taxes from the fish merchant." Everybody wins in this situation. Well, aside from the merchant.

12
VÍREO

"*Monsters are former men and women forced into a darkened place where they pledge their bodies to the gods in some form of twisted trade. The gods do not always answer but when they do, they act with twisted intentions.*"

-Jordell Torvin, Legends of Levanthria, 260 KR

Before the war, the Great Temple was where people came to pray to their gods and donate their coin for their causes. Now the temple is in complete decay. Tiles on each of the four spires are missing, and two of them are crumbling halfway down. The stonework is covered in thick green moss reaching as far up as the upper stained-glass windows, the stories they once told muted and dishevelled. What remains is unsightly at the very least, and the less time we spend here, the better. I guess the people have lost faith, blaming their gods for their hardships. But it isn't the gods that come to collect their coins.

The smell of the slums seems to get worse every time

we visit. Death, rotting food, and sewage blend to make a horrific stench that burns the nostrils. I pull the top of my tunic over my nose. My cologne only partially keeps the smell at bay.

Outside the temple, a man is tending to a young woman who cradles an infant in her arms.

"Please, can you help him? He grows limp." The woman is frantic. Her clothes are ripped and covered in mud. I assume she and her baby are homeless.

"Take this, child." The balding man passes the woman some bread and a small bottle. "The bread to replenish yourself so you can feed your child. Drink the vial one hour before feeding her and she will be better before you know it." He smiles at her and places a reassuring hand over hers.

"Oh, thank you! Bless you!"

"No need to thank me. It is why I am here."

The woman scurries away, and the balding man see us. His robes, which appear to be made from old potato sacks sewn together, seem to engulf his slim frame. The sleeves have been cut out roughly and parts of the hem drag on the ground.

His eyes meet mine and he makes a face of disgust before turning away to climb the steps behind him.

"Jordell!" I call out. "I suggest you stop, alchemist. I do not have time for this."

"I'd listen to him," Lek bellows, his voice echoing around the open space like a horn. "No need for this to get nasty, is there?" Jordell ignores us and shuffles inside.

"Lord Jareb sent us." I can feel my impatience rising. I just want my reward so that we can return to my manor to drink and feast on deer.

Jordell stops in his tracks. He hesitates, then gestures for us to follow him into the temple. His hard expression shows me that we do not intimidate him, but one does not refuse an order from King Almerion's own steward.

Lek and I accompany Jordell through the rusting, iron-clad door which looks as if it is ready to fall from its hinges. Gillam stays outside to watch over our cart.

My skin crawls as we enter the building. The usual orderly rows of benches have been replaced with about thirty makeshift beds, all of which are filled with people. Most of the patients are elderly, but there are younger men and women, too. A thin child sits by his mother's bedside, his face in his hands.

The groans and coughs of the unwell fill the ceremonial chamber, and there is a small handful of members of the Great Temple who tend to the sick that litter the hall, their robes heavily frayed. Everyone is in desperate need of a wash.

Jordell leads us to the far end of the hall and into a back chamber. When we step inside, it is fresh air compared to the hall of the ill. Lek gasps as he removes his tunic from his face.

"Rather dramatic, don't you think?" Jordell glares at Lek. "People in this part of town are sick and dying. They need food and clean water. Any money they had has been taken from them. Those unable to pay their taxes have lost their homes."

I clear my throat. I didn't come here to listen to Jordell's mewling. "That is all very well, but Jareb has asked us to fetch you immediately."

Jordell's eyes have turned to anger and his body is tense. "You have the nerve to walk in here like you own the place, like you are above all these lives!" He slams his fist onto his desk.

"With all due respect, we are. Perhaps you are not familiar with my title?" I need to put this man in his place.

"How dare you!" The alchemist picks up a book from his desk and launches it at me. I duck out of the way and raise my hands in surrender.

"It's because of *you* that the people have no coin left, no homes to shelter their loved ones," he seethes, jabbing his finger in the air towards me. "It is you that is the illness, Vireo! I know very well who you are. The only reason I have allowed you in this building is because Jareb has commanded it, and we cannot afford to lose this temple!" He stands with his fists clenched.

"I mean no harm, alchemist." I can't help but feel that my words are falling on deaf ears. "Everything we do, we do for the crown. To assist with the war."

"All the while, you sit in your fancy manor with your servants, your fine wines, feasts, and silk. Do not fool yourself. You help no one but yourself, Vireo. You are a vain man who will always put yourself before others." Spit leaves his mouth as he speaks. Now I am the one with clenched fists.

Lek grabs my arm and casts me a firm look, before turning to the alchemist. "Please forgive us, Jordell, we mean you no harm."

"Harm is, however, a consequence of your presence wherever you three go."

I wouldn't normally allow someone to speak to us with such grave disrespect, but we are here on official orders, so I abstain from my urge to pummel him.

Lek stands firm, maintaining his composure in the face of insolence. "We have a request from Lord Jareb," he says calmly. "If you listen, you may be able to help end the war and the poverty. You have a chance to end the suffering here."

Jordell dusts down his ruffled tunic and sits. "Go on?"

"We have come across a book. A spell book," Lek says.

Jordell sighs, but it seems his interest is piqued. "And you need *me* to interpret it, I presume?"

Nodding, Lek continues, "The Zarubians are using magic against our armies."

"But that cannot be possible. It is unheard of for someone to wield magic in an offensive way." Jordell leans across his desk. "Do you have it with you? The book?"

I withdraw the book from my satchel and place it in front of him. Looking apprehensive, he unwraps it slowly, then opens it to reveal the unknown language. His eyes skim frantically over the pages.

"You are right, this is a spell book. Even if I could somehow translate this, you would need a strong mage to carry out the enchantments. It's unlikely you'll find a mage to be very forthcoming. Not when they fetch such high prices as slaves."

"Jareb has ordered that any enslaved mages must be allowed to work for the crown," I inform him. "He is also offering to pay them for their services."

"Still, I don't know that they'd just submit to the crown. They have been ostracized for too long."

"Jareb wants to reward anyone who comes forward with freedom and coin, so that they can train and harness their skills," I continue.

"And who will teach them?" Jordell presses me.

"You will, of course," I tell him, but he still looks uncertain. "Jareb knows you are a skilled alchemist. You will be entrusted with secrets to the crown. You can help end this war." I hope this is enough to sway him, because I refuse to beg a man in rags.

Jareb considers this thoughtfully. "Promise supplies for

me to tend to these people, and I will do it. I want you to give me your word and your honour," he says.

I grit my teeth, feeling that Jareb better reward me well for my efforts. "You have my word."

The plan is set in motion. Now all we need to do is wait.

Outside, Gillam is waiting for us by the cart. She has her hand tucked into her tunic, clasping her dagger. This can only mean one thing: she is ready to strike.

Lek does not appear to have noticed and continues his walk to the cart, whistling a tune. Gillam meets my eyes and then nods her head, indicating towards my right.

It is none other than Orjan, the man who has owed me money for the past three weeks. He is in full plate armour and he clutches his helmet under his arm, his blonde hair matted from wearing it. He is a strong, athletic man with a medium-sized frame. The yellow and gold cloth draped over his armour represents the kingdom of Rashouya, from which he hails.

Orjan is speaking with a boy who is no older than fifteen. It appears the two of them have been sparring. With any luck, Orjan will have exerted himself and reduced his chances of running.

Each time I have approached Orjan these past few weeks, he has given new excuses for why he cannot pay me. I have grown tired of his excuses. Which means he is going to learn this the hard way. If there is one thing I despise more than anything, it is people not paying money owed to me. I am not a charitable man.

"Orjan!" I bellow, my voice carrying across the space between us. His gaze meets mine, and to my surprise, he does not run. He points to the boy, who shuffles back away from him. I can tell by Orjan's armour that he has a squire now, and I cannot help but wonder how he is paying him.

"Vireo, I do not wish to quarrel." His Rashouyan accent betrays his southern roots.

"There is no quarrel here," I start, "providing you have the coin that you owe me."

"It is here." He walks over to his horse and removes a small purse. He then approaches me tentatively, halving the distance between us before throwing the bag in my direction. I catch it and pass it to Lek, who counts the contents.

"It's what he owes from the card game," Lek grumbles in my ear. "His debt is paid."

"Where is the interest, Orjan?" I call out. I hear Lek sigh.

"Interest? Vireo, I settled the debt. I want no quarrel," Orjan reiterates.

"Then you should have paid on time." I walk towards Orjan, and Lek and Gillam follow at my heel. I place my hand in the air to signal for them to stop. I've made my decision.

Orjan retrieves his morning star from his side – a weapon with a metal shaft fixed to a spiked metal ball. I unsheathe my sword and speed towards him, the dirt crunching beneath my feet. I swing my blade, but Orjan has adopted a defensive stance and easily parries my attack.

"We do not need to do this, Vireo."

I swing again and again with Orjan blocking each blow. Then he spots an opening and crashes his morning star into my armour, knocking me sideways. The pain is bearable; nothing that some quick breaths can't allow me to get through. I laugh to myself as I juggle my blade from hand to hand, then conduct a flurry of attacks with my sword. Orjan blocks each one with relative ease. I hate fighting a defensive opponent. It makes the job so much harder.

But I have a strategy, and a few parried strikes later, I have figured out his fighting style. I strike from above twice, which Orjan deflects, and then I swing my sword to his right. He blocks this before thrashing his morning star at my side again. This time, I have read the move. I grab the shaft of his weapon – something I would not be able to do if he were wielding a blade – and stop his attack in an instant. Stepping forward into his personal space, I pummel his face with a single blow from the hilt of my sword. As he staggers backwards, his nose explodes with blood, which splatters across my face. My anger still grips me, and I step forward and hit him again. The third time, he falls.

"Orjan!" the boy cries from the side, tears forming in his eyes.

"Stay there, boy," he calls back through a mouthful of blood.

I kick Orjan's morning star from his hand and stand over him, pointing my sword at his throat.

"I yield," he says through rasping breaths. The broken nose seems to make it difficult for him to breathe, so I offer him a hand to sit up, which he accepts.

"I do not want to see you in this city again, Orjan." I walk away from him.

"You do not have that jurisdiction over me!" He calls in defiance. Is he really that stupid?

"Maybe you just need some persuasion, then." I nod at Lek and Gillam, who rush towards Orjan and begin beating him furiously as I make my way back to the cart.

13
VIREO

My chamber is dark as I enter in my robes. It has been a long day, but a hot bath washed away the stench that clung to me like an unwanted embrace, and I am pleasantly full from the succulent venison that my staff prepared for dinner. Choa is a fine cook, and I am glad to have her in my ranks.

The candles bring a pleasant glow to the room, and I sit on the edge of my bed, thinking about the day. I hope that Jareb's plan will work, as I grow tired of collecting money all day. I wish to go back to how things used to be. I can only hope that the alchemist is as skilled at transcribing as he apparently is at making potions.

A cold draught blows against my back. Looking around the room in surprise, I see nothing. Then for a second, the candles in the room dance.

My heart skips. I am not alone. Somebody has opened the window – and I know it was shut only moments before. I reach for the blade on my bed and unsheathe it.

"Who is there?" I call out. I will slay anyone that wishes me harm, especially someone with the nerve to trespass into my home. The curtains continue to blow in the breeze, and the candlelight dances around me. Maybe it's just my paranoia. Half the city would gladly see me hang for my role as a collector. But I do whatever I must to maintain the lifestyle I live. I refuse to lose the home that has been in my family for generations, and I certainly do not wish to become accustomed to living without the luxuries I so enjoy.

Hands reach around me from behind. I raise my sword, ready to strike.

"Now, now, my love. Is that any way to treat a lady?" Her softly spoken voice entrances me instantly. The snake charmer.

"Allana?"

"Who else would it be?" She prolongs each word that she speaks.

I turn around. She is wearing a long green tunic with the hood up to hide her appearance, but the smell of her perfume easily confirms her identity. "What are you doing here? You can't sneak out of the castle at this time. Someone will raise the alarm."

Raising her head, her piercing green eyes meet mine and I cannot remove my gaze from her. I feel frozen, unable to move. "But it is ok for you to sneak into my chambers whenever you wish to have me?" She strokes her hand up my chest playfully before reaching for her hood to lower it. "I grew tired of waiting for you, so I thought tonight I would come here and claim you instead, like you have so often claimed me."

In my head, I scream at her recklessness. Her thrill-seeking behaviour will get us both killed. But it is this side of her that drew me in from the start. She hooked me in like a fish, and now I cannot let go of the bait. "You are tempting fate, Allana. Do you not care for our heads? First you placed your hand on my shoulder in front of your husband, and now this."

"But did your heart not race, my love?"

She is a tease, one that I cannot get enough of. I could easily have any woman in Levanthria, but I have become obsessed with Allana. She is all I can think about at times.

"It is racing now." I pull her towards me and we embrace, her soft lips pressing against mine. I breathe in her perfume, wishing we could stay in this moment for as long as possible. I feel for her like I have never felt for any other woman. I wish I did not have to share her with her useless husband.

"You can't stay, Allana, as much I might want it. And trust me, I do. But if your husband notices you missing, it will be the end of us both."

"You are already trying to get rid of me?"

The temptation is setting in and I feel my heart banging against my chest like a drum. In this instance, however, I must think with my head. "If they catch us . . . Allana, this is madness."

"It is so monotonous at the castle, Vireo. I need excitement. I need you. What if I don't go back?"

"Then I would be dead by the morning."

"I mean it, Vireo. What if I were to leave the castle, and Levanthria? Would you come with me? Would you give up all this for me?" She is teasing again, talking in a playful manner, trying to entice me into an answer. In truth, though, the offer is tempting. I am tired of this city, and with the coin I have stored, we could start a new life.

"In a heartbeat," I tell her. Allana is the only woman I have ever been honest with.

"Then let's do it." Her eyes are wide with excitement.

"How long have we been sharing a bed with one another now?"

"Not long enough." I pull her in for another embrace, which she succumbs to.

"I mean it, Vireo. I cannot bear the castle any longer."

She is being serious, but so am I. I would gladly leave to be with her. If leaving Levanthria is what it takes, then I will do it.

"Then make preparations, Allana," I tell her. "Tomorrow night, we leave Levanthria for good."

14

JAREB

" I have searched far and wide, stalking the plains of Levanthria in search of the legends behind the stories. Some think these were created in order to teach their children the ways of the world. If only they knew the truth."
-Gregor Yerald, Monsters and Myths, 256 KR

I am finding my whirling thoughts hard to shake. There is so much riding on Jordell being able to transcribe that spell book. It feels inconceivable that we could have an army of mages at our disposal before long, but I pray my plan will bear fruit.

There was a fleeting moment during that meeting with Vireo and his thugs when Allana laid her hand on Vireo's shoulder. The image of that small gesture has repeated itself in my mind ever since I parted company with that wretched excuse of a man.

I am alone in our bed. Allana sometimes likes to walk the gardens in the evening, for fresh air, but I am often too tired to join her. I try to banish my thoughts; I am being ridiculous. Allana and I have been married for five years now. I know I am older than her, but I try to please her as best as I can, even though I feel unworthy of her affections.

I can feel the storm brewing in my head – that moment at the meeting was nothing but a passing graze. I love Allana with all my heart, and I cannot imagine her doing anything to betray my trust in her.

I clench my jaw and anger rises in me. If that beast has laid one finger on her, I do not know how I may react. What I wouldn't give to put that vermin in his place and wipe that smug grin from his face.

I am just being paranoid, I tell myself once more.

But what if I am not?

15
VIREO

The sky is black. I pace outside the castle walls going over the plan in my head, preparing for a life-changing decision. I know it's the right one – to hell with whatever anyone else thinks.

Lek and Gillam were less than impressed with the plan, but after I promised them my manor and my land, they seemed to fall back in line. Now they have both reluctantly offered to help me with my plan. The three of us have been through a lot together. After tonight, I may never see them again.

"Vireo!" Gillam hisses at me through gritted teeth. "You are making me nervous. Stop pacing around like a wild legonna before you draw attention to us!"

I glance back over my shoulder at Lek and Gillam, who sit side by side at the front of my cart, my brothers in arms. Gillam, the master thief – her skills are unlike any other in her field. Her ability to hide in the shadows and strike when least expected has always made her a formidable ally. With her dark attire, she is barely visible, hidden in Lek's hulking shadow.

Lek wears heavy armour, and his great axe is strapped to his back. The only thing he is missing to complete his resemblance of a bear are the claws. He looks as wild as they come, but out of the three of us, he has always been the calmest.

They both advised me earlier this very evening how stupid I was being when I told them of my plan to flee Levanthria with Allana. It took a good hour for Gillam to stop throwing things at me and Lek to stop sulking.

"Remember the plan," I whisper to them both through the shadows.

"It isn't difficult to remember." Lek's words are short, a sign that his more diplomatic nature is wavering.

While Lek and Gillam wait in the cart, I'm supposed to climb the castle wall.

"Okay," I say. "I'm doing it."

I lean my head to the side and click my neck loudly, gathering my courage for the ascent. The castle wall must be at least two hundred feet high. I take about fifty steps back, then I retrieve an arrow from my quill, which I have tied a rope to.

This is a ridiculous shot to even attempt, but I know in my heart that with my bow, I cannot miss. I never do. The bow has been in my family for generations, and I have trained with it since I was just a boy. And now it all comes down to this moment. I trust this weapon more than I trust Lek and Gillam. When I use it, I can do the impossible.

I take a deep breath and draw the bow back, focussing on the wooden beam that protrudes from the castle wall just below the top. This is the target.

I gaze at the spot, waiting for the feeling to take me – the one when I know to release the arrow. Then, I let loose, and the arrow soars through the air, the rope trailing behind it like a ribbon. It dances behind the arrow for a few seconds until I hear a soft thud, and I know it has made contact with the beam above me.

I tug on the rope with force to ensure it is embedded. Two hundred feet is a long way to fall. A gentle wind makes the grass rustle around me. I make my way to the dark cold wall, and take another deep breath.

"Wish me luck," I whisper to Lek and Gillam before beginning the steep ascent to the top.

16

JAREB

A flash enters my dreams, warming me as if I sit by the fire. It kisses my face to comfort me before piercing my mind like a knife into butter.

"Wake up," an unknown voice hisses at me, snake-like. It is loud enough to startle me awake and I sit bolt upright, my heart drumming against my chest.

It is the dead of night, and my bed feels cold. I lean over for Allana but find she is not here. I am startled by this, and the words that woke me are forgotten in an instant. All I want is to show her my affection, how much she means to me. Maybe I've been neglecting my marital duties, given the burden I carry on my shoulders. Most days are a struggle now, when each decision I must make helps the war but causes the people of Askela to despise me.

I make my way to the balcony, where the light of the moon glows through the large glass doors. I step outside and breathe in the refreshing, cold air. Then a sharp pain engulfs my mind, forcing my eyes to bind shut. I clasp my hands against my temple and my eyes stream from the strain. I fear that if I am not careful, I risk falling from the balcony.

"*Wake up!*" The hissing voice has a feminine undertone to it, but it is more serpentine than human.

"*Lady Allana makes to run away!*" The voice in my mind hisses, each word piercing my ear as if someone shouts in proximity, causing me to wince. Am I dreaming?

I feel my heart sink to the pit of my stomach. Have I lost my mind? My hands shake uncontrollably, the invading words further confirming my suspicions. After all, where is Allana? I have every right to be concerned.

"*She makes to leave with Vireo. Find them!*" The noise of the voice is unbearable, its aggression worsening.

"Vireo!?" Feeling that my legs may give away from underneath me, I steady myself against the balcony. Allana is my all, my everything. The one shining beacon of light in this treacherous city that keeps me going, keeps me from losing my sanity. The pain I am feeling is unbearable, like nothing I have ever experienced. It quickly turns to rage.

Outside my bedchambers, I call for the guards, but when I step into the hall, I find that my sentries lie on the floor unconscious. Could the hissing warning be true?

I set off running down the hallway, the stone floor freezing against my bare feet. My heart is racing. I do not know where I run, only that I must find them and stop this madness. All I can see in my mind is the smug face of Vireo laughing at me. How long has this been going on? How long have they played me for a fool? How many others know about this affair? I continue to shout for the guards, and four come trotting to my side.

"Sire?" One of them asks, confused at the state I am in.

"Allana!" I shout. "We must find Allana!"

The soldiers follow behind me as I frantically search the

halls. We must find them. I will not let them get away with this.

"This way sir, they are heading for the courtyard!" A voice calls. Soldiers head that way, their ranks growing in numbers. I follow.

17
VIREO

There is all manner of dark creatures that exist in this world. A woman, tethered to a loch, exacting her revenge. An ice golem far to the north, wandering the plains, slaughtering anything that crosses its path. A lady of the night, her headless body said to roam the Mouth of Antar, her will unknown. These are just a few that I track, wanting to uncover the history behind them. Most fear them, but I wish to help them, to free them from their curses.

-Gregor Yerald, Monsters and Myths, 264 KR

This seemed like such a good plan at the time. Now I am questioning our stupidity. It started off well. I scaled the castle walls, then made my way to Jareb and Allana's bedchamber. I dispatched the guards quickly and quietly, rendering them both unconscious. Allana exited the chambers and left with me. She came out in her emerald-green overcoat with the hood up, whispering to me that it was the darkest clothing she had.

Now, just as we make our way towards the courtyard, a

guard spots us and calls out. Allana's hand grips mine as we run, but it is nearly impossible to keep hold of her soft velvet gloves.

The blood is coursing through my veins, and I feel like my chest is about to explode as we rush towards our freedom. Not long now before we will start our new life together, away from Askela.

"We are not going to make it!" Allana yells.

"We are almost there."

Allana cries out as she stumbles, hitting the floor of the courtyard. I jolt to a stop, my momentum sliding me through the gravel as I rush to help Allana to her feet. She grabs my hand, panic-stricken.

"I've got you," I tell her.

"Promise me we'll make it, Vireo."

"I promise."

For a moment, we crouch behind a cluster of barrels on the edge of the courtyard, waiting. We can hear shouts, but the courtyard seems clear and I know this is our chance to make a break for it. We must get to the gates on the other side, where Gillam and Lek are waiting.

We seize our opportunity.

"Let's go," I command, and we set off at pace, the gravel crunching underneath our feet, and I know we are going to make it, that we are going to be ok.

Something trips me, and I hit the ground with such force that all the air escapes my lungs. Allana screams. I see stars as I look at my feet to find that they have been bound with weighted rope thrown from afar.

"Keep going, Allana!" I tell her as I retrieve the dagger in my boot and start hacking. But the guards are already upon me, and I am outnumbered by three to one. I attempt to reach for my sword just as one soldier lunges for me. I plunge the dagger into his chest and slam him into the ground before spinning on my knees with my sword outstretched, slicing into another guard's legs. He shrieks out in agony as he falls to the ground into a pool of blood that he shares with his colleague. The third guard dives at me, incensed at seeing his comrades felled. I flick my sword up towards him and drive the blade through his stomach, and he slides down the metal, his weight pinning me to the ground.

"Vireo!" I hear Allana call out, but I do not see her. I hoist the guard off me, rolling out of the way just in time to avoid a blow that rains down in my direction. I kick out and leg sweep the man, bringing him to the floor before jumping on top of him, and I proceed to beat his face with my fists. Someone pulls me backwards, and I struggle against the grip, but the men behind me hold me in place and kick the backs of my knees.

The escape is over. We have failed. The guards part in front of me and Jareb passes through them in his red gilded night robe. I try to find Allana, but as I turn, I feel a blow to my head.

Jareb stands before me, breathing heavily, his fists clenched.

His face is contorted with rage.

This can't end well.

18

JAREB

A rush of anger fills me, and I strike Vireo in the face as hard as I can. He looks unfazed by the blow, and for a second, I swear he smirks at me. I hit him a second time, and this time his blood splatters across the gravel from a burst lip.

"How dare you!" I strike him a third time. This time, crimson streams down his face and it is deeply satisfying. I have wanted to do that for so long.

Vireo spits the pooling blood in his mouth onto the floor and attempts to stare me down, but I do not waver. I have the power here, but somehow, I still feel helpless.

"You had to take her!" I shout. "The one thing I treasured the most, and you could not leave her alone. You had to have *her*, out of all the women in this kingdom." I can feel my anger rising to a level like never before. A fire rages within my soul. Why is it always me that ends up worse off, despite my best efforts to please everyone, no matter how hard I try? Meanwhile, Vireo walks around like an arrogant cock, and despite his selfishness, despite the fact that he will always put his wants and wishes before any other, people worship the ground he walks on.

My eyes burn and tears fall from my face onto the gravel. "Why have you done this to me? To us? You should have let her be."

Vireo looks up at me in bloody defiance. "I love her." His words hit me like an arrow in the chest. He speaks of love, but I know he cannot love any person other than himself.

"LOVE!" I cry. "You do not know what love is, Vireo. If you did, you would not have led Allana to a fool's escape."

"Stop, my love," Allana's voice says gently. The guards have brought her back. They grip her arms tightly, and I do not feel like instructing them to let go. I'm not even sure whether she's speaking to me, or Vireo.

"Don't you dare, Allana," I scold her, and she has the decency to drop her gaze to the floor in shame. Her betrayal is unforgivable, and I know what I must do.

"Take her to the dungeon." I cannot bear to look at her. She has never looked uglier to me. After everything I have done for her, this is how she thanks me.

The guards march her forward against Allana's futile struggles. She does not have the strength to fight them off, and her feet slide across the stone.

"No, you can't!" She emits a frantic cry like a panic-stricken animal. "Unhand me, my love, please." Her words are to no avail. Allana cannot change her fate.

"You can rot in the dungeons for all I care," I say.

"Please my love, I beg you."

I continue to ignore her empty words while I stare at Vireo, still undecided about how I am going to seal his fate.

"I'M WITH CHILD!"

The courtyard falls silent, and the searing pain behind

my eyes returns, making it impossible for me to concentrate.

"*Do not fall for her lies.*" The voice hisses as clear as day, its words sounding as if the speaker is in pain. No one else reacts to it. How is this voice only speaking to me?

"My love, you – you are the father."

"*Lies.*" The anger in the disembodied voice startles me.

She really is desperate. I can't bring myself to look at her, such is my disgust at the vile steps she is taking to avoid the dungeons. Little does she know, she has sealed her fate with her claim; I have a secret that I have never shared with her.

I stare at Vireo, and I see a genuine sadness in his eyes. Did he know she was with child?

"STOP!" I yell to the guards, looking at Allana. "You are with child?" She is shaking from head to foot, terrified for her life.

"Yes. I am with your child."

"*Punish her,*" the voice commands, "*Show her what happens to those who wrong you.*"

I fight to stop myself from responding out loud. The last thing I need now is for the guards to see that Levanthria's steward has lost his mind. The pressure in my head is unbearable. My hands are shaking with rage as I struggle with darkened thoughts of what I wish to do to my wife.

"*You long for people to respect you. Punish her and you will see, people will listen. People will take notice.*" The voice stutters, its words fragmented and painful.

I feel that my mind snaps, like a rope with too much tension. A volcanic rage rises from deep within, ready to erupt. Years of suppressed feelings burst to the front of my mind, and any affection I had for Allana shatters completely.

"LIES!"

"You see, Allana, I cannot create children, something which I have never shared with you. It is impossible for me to be a father." My words are true. It is a fact confirmed by a healer. I felt shame when I was first told, so I kept it to myself because I could not bear to crush our dreams of having children. Now I feel nothing but disgust and anger. She would happily have had me think this child was mine.

"Destroy them!" The voice in my mind commands.

Allana's face falls as she seems to realise the reality of her situation. Her skin blotches with purple patches from her forced tears.

It is time for me to show people what it means to cross me.

19

VÍREO

My face throbs from the blows, but my heart aches more. Can it be true that Allana carries my child? Why hasn't she told me? Is this why she suddenly wants to flee?

I don't have time to ponder this further, because Jareb grabs hold of Allana's arm and drags her towards me. There is madness in his eyes as he stands her level with me.

"I will get us out of this," I try to reassure her.

Her eyes are flooded with tears, and it kills me that there is nothing I can do. I lunge at Jareb, but the guards hold me in place.

"If you hurt her, I'll kill you," I say, gritting my teeth. I mean every word that I speak.

Jareb fixes his stare on me again, his eyes reddened and vacant.

"You make a valid point, Víreo." His words feel twisted, barbed like thorns. "I am led to believe that you are an excellent shot with your bow. In fact, I have heard that you never miss." He seizes Allana by the hair and drags her to the other side of the courtyard. This is unlike Jareb. I have never witnessed or heard tales of such aggression and callousness from him. Our actions have truly broken him.

"Guards, fetch the targets for practice."

What is he doing? Two guards drag over an archery target and he stands Allana in front of it, whispering something into her ear.

Then it dawns on me, and I am filled with horror.

"Take one step forward, and I will slit her throat," Jareb says. "Mark my words, Vireo." Then he nods to the guards, and they release me, but I don't feel free.

"You have a target. I want you to hit it three times." The way he moves and speaks has changed. His eyes twitch, and he gestures with jerking motions, as if someone else stands beside him. "Yes, three times," he mutters, as if talking to himself, descending into madness. "If you hit the target three times, then I will grant you both your freedom to leave the kingdom and never come back." His words are bitter. "Shoot at anything other than this target and I will see to it that your manor, your family titles, and your friends are all burned to the ground. I will see to it that your family's lineage is removed from history as if it never existed."

I do not know if he means his words. I have my bow, so I know I will not miss. I quickly load an arrow and fire as fast as I can. I want to get this sick game over and done with so we can leave. The arrow lands in the target to the left of Allana's head, who flinches. She screams, looking ready to faint. I know if I fire quickly, I have a better chance of success.

"No, no, no, that will simply not do, Vireo. I have heard that's the bow you never miss with. Using it simply gives you too much of an advantage."

The guards snatch away my bow, and I feel like I have lost a limb.

"Will someone pass him a replacement? The man has another two shots to make." He is goading me.

I panic. I have not used another bow for so long. A newfound doubt creeps over me like a shadow, and my confidence fades like the setting sun. A guard forces a new weapon into my hand. The feel of it is completely foreign to me.

I load an arrow and draw it back, holding my breath as I focus on the target.

Please don't let me hit her. I exhale and release. Allana screams again as the arrow buries itself in the target beside her. Her sleeve darkens with blood from her fresh wound. I realise with horror that I have nicked the outside of her arm.

Only one more shot to go, and we can leave.

"Please, my love, please stop." Allana's chest heaves with frantic sobs.

"Keep silent and still, Allana. " I am surprised by the tremble in my voice.

"Hurry up, Vireo."

My hands shake as I nock the final arrow. Eyes burn into me like a searing poker, and I want the ground to swallow me up. What if I nick Allana again? Focusing on the outer edges of the target, I know that this is what I need to hit. The shake in my hand is getting worse, however. I need to take this shot quickly before my nerves conquer me completely. Seconds feel like an eternity. Then I release the arrow.

There is a dull thud. Allana's eyes widen as she looks down. I recoil in horror.

I have embedded the arrow into her chest.

Her green overcoat turns crimson as she begins to bleed out.

She looks up at me briefly. "I love you," she says. Then her eyes close, never to open again.

The grief hits me like a battering ram, and my throat burns as I scream.

What have I done?

20

VIREO

To the southwest of the Biterian Plains sits the Mouth of Antar, a large hole within the ground said to lead to a network of underground tunnels. It is said to be here that the headless woman roams, and that within these tunnels her body lies. I intend to find her.

-Gregor Yerald, monster hunter and explorer, 266 KR

My legs buckle and I drop to the floor. I have killed her. I have snuffed out the flame of the one thing in the world I valued more than myself.

The child. Oh god, the unborn child. *My* unborn child.

Time stands still as I stare at Allana's motionless body. I feel numb, as if my soul is draining from my body.

It takes me a few minutes to realise that chaos has erupted around me.

"Get up, Vireo!" The muffled words barely reach me. "Blasts, get up!" I feel a slap around the back of my head, which brings me back. A hulking figure stands beside me; Lek grips his bloodied great axe.

69

A guard rushes us. Lek flips the man over his shoulder like he is made of cotton, then spins and slams his axe down into the man's chest. A fountain of blood sprays Lek's armour, and I feel the warmth of it as it splashes against my face.

Lek removes his axe from the guard on the floor just as another is upon us. He steps forward and greets the oncoming guard with the heel of his foot, hurtling him backwards.

"Get up, Vireo!" He growls at me again, "We need to get out." He offers a hand to me, which I take, and he drags me to my feet.

Gillam tears her way through guards as if ripping through parchment. Her flurry of attacks easily take down the guards that surround her. I count at least seven either dead or injured on the ground at her feet as she continues to dance her way through them, slicing with the precision of a viper. Through the chaos, I see Jareb standing by Allana's body, brushing her hair back behind her ear.

Rage takes over, and all I feel is hatred. I lose all sense of self as I set off at speed through the ensuing battle towards my enemy. When a guard steps into my path, I smash his face with the bow in my hand so hard that my weapon snaps in two. The force sends the guard stumbling backwards. I reach for an arrow from my quiver and burrow it deep into his eye. Nothing is getting in my way.

Jareb has seen me coming and is waiting for me with sword in hand. I grab a blade from the guard I have just dispatched and the two of us lock eyes on one another.

I make to move towards him, but someone clasps my shoulder, holding me in place.

"Vireo, we must leave!" Lek is not asking for permission.

"Let me go!"

But now a handful of guards form a protective barrier around Jareb.

I struggle against Lek, but the man is a beast, and he holds me in place despite my best efforts to force him off me. The thought of using my sword against him crosses my mind. Jareb is ushered into the castle and the doors shut behind him. My opportunity for vengeance is gone.

"At least let me see Allana, you oaf!" My voice is cracked and broken. Lek releases me and I sprint across the courtyard. He follows, providing me with protective cover, while Gillam makes her way towards us, guards at her heel.

Gravel sprays as I reach Allana's body, and I purse her face in my hands. Her cheeks are cold and wet with the tears she had been crying when I ended her life.

"Allana, I am so sorry. This is all my fault."

Lek and Gillam form behind me and fend off the guards.

I kiss her on her head and breathe in her honey-infused perfume, brushing my hand down her cheek. Her emerald green hood is torn off, most likely from when Jareb dragged her to the archery target.

"Come on, Vireo, we must leave," Gillam urges. "We cannot fight them off all day."

I place one last tender kiss on Allana's lips. Then, I grab the hood and pull the cloak from her, knowing that it will bear her scent. It is all I have left of her now.

Lek pulls me back away from her and points. "Head for the gate. I will open it. GO!"

All three of us set across the courtyard where fallen guards lie dead or wounded. Those that are still alive groan through their injuries. We spilled a lot of blood today, and we will lose our heads if we're caught.

We reach the gate. Lek disappears to the side and within a moment, it starts to rise.

"That will do, Lek!" Gillam calls out, and the gate grinds to a halt. More guards are forming behind us. We lunge beneath the iron and make haste for the cart.

Lek and Gillam jump into the back, and I take the reins.

"Yah!" I lash the back of the horses and they set off at a gallop, the back wheels bouncing as they hit mounds and rocks on the ground. I do not have to look behind us to know that mounted guards will be in pursuit. The cart gains momentum as we hurtle towards town. I can hear the rallying cries of soldiers giving chase on their steeds. They will have speed on their side because they are not lugging a cart behind them.

"Blasts, Vireo, speed up! They are on us!" Lek yells. The cart shudders as Lek swings out his axe to startle one of the advancing guards.

The darkness makes it hard to see where we are going, but I can make out the illuminated outer gates of the city walls before long, the cart now moving at incredible speed. Two guards move to block our path, but when they see that we have no intention of stopping, they dive out of the way just in time to avoid being crumpled under our wheels.

All we have now is the glow from the moonlight to guide our path, and we leave the dirt track, into the darkness. The cart bobs up and down on uneven ground.

"Vireo, where are you heading?" Gillam shouts.

Lek growls, "Don't even think about it!"

"We have no choice; we can lose them in the woods." I know that entering the Forest of Opiya is a stupid idea, but for now, it is our only option.

I feel a tug on my shoulder and realise that Lek has tried to pull me backwards, away from the reins. He might have succeeded but at that moment, the cart ricochets off a bump in our path, causing him to lose his balance.

"You're mad, Vireo!" He bellows at me.

The shouts of the guards are fading; they have seen sense and have stopped their pursuit.

"I'd rather take my chances with them! Stop the cart!" Gillam yells. Both are less than happy with my decision, but at least we are alive. For now.

21

JAREB

I sit at my desk, lost in bitter thoughts. My parchment is sodden with tears. I need to inform the king of his niece's death, something that I am sure he will not take kindly to. For this reason, I do not share the full details of last night's events. Placing my hands against my head, I massage my temple to ease my throbbing pain.

I am grief-stricken by Allana's passing, even if it was me that instigated her last moments. I sob as I write the words, informing the king that she has been murdered by the now outlawed Vireo. Words that I believe to be true.

I hate her for what she has done, for what she has forced me to do. I will not tolerate further disrespect from anyone. No longer will I be pitied, no longer will I let others make a fool out of me, laughing at me while my back is turned. For now on, they will fear me, or face the consequences when they cross me. I will bring my fury down upon any who have taken advantage of my good will.

Vireo somehow got away last night. Like the animal that he is, he headed for the woodlands. More fool him. It brings me comfort knowing that Vireo is in the Forest of

Opiya. Before long, he will either be driven to madness or killed by one of the many creatures that reside there. Vireo and his rodent thugs will wish that we had captured them by the time the forest is through with them.

While I am certain that the woodlands will take care of them, I have placed a thirty-coin bounty on their heads. Twenty for Vireo and five each for Lek and Gillam to the man or woman who brings me their heads. Double if they are brought back to me alive.

I finish my letter, the last words smudged by my tears. If only that man had not come into our lives, my sweet Allana would not have been corrupted. He forced my hand.

I press my signet ring into red wax to seal the letter shut. The deep red of the lion and snake intertwined remind me of the blood spilled last night.

There is a brisk knock on the door.

"Enter," I call.

The door creaks and a timid-looking messenger boy pokes his head through the small gap, his face and ruffled, matted hair are blackened with filth from the city.

"Sire, there is a someone claiming to be a mage waiting for you in the Great Hall."

At least something good may come from today.

"Take this and see that it is sent to the king." I stand from the desk and pass him the parchment with one hand and a coin from the other.

"Thank you, sire." The boy's bright blue eyes light up and he snatches both from me before running off down the corridor.

The Great Hall is grand in every way. Large pillars form columns on the outer edges of the white polished stone, carved to form spirals all the way to the top. The base of each pillar blends in with the ground as if the room has been carved from one large stone connecting to the speckled, marble floor.

Portraits of former kings, queens, and regents adorn the walls, as well as brass plaques intricately detailing their feats. At the head of the hall sits the largest stained-glass window in the castle. The form of the goddess Opiya has been delicately put together with the brightly coloured glass. She is holding her hand below her to the ground, as if raising trees where she points. The sunlight shines through, making the image even more mesmerising and divine as it produces an aura around her.

I wonder if my feats will be remembered, or if my legacy will be swallowed up and spit out by the grandness of this hall.

A woman stands in wait for me, and I cannot help but feel bemused. She wears a blue gown and has a slender figure, one that I cannot help but admire from behind. She almost catches me in stare when she turns around to face me. Her vibrant, wild red curls fall to her shoulders, and her hazel eyes and smile are sharp and alluring.

"My lord." The woman curtsies so elegantly that she looks as though she is hovering in the air.

I shake myself from my stupor. "I'm sorry, my lady – it is just that I was told a mage was waiting to see me." For the messenger boy's sake, I hope he was not lying to me in order to gain some quick coin.

The woman laughs delicately and brings her hand to her mouth, feigning surprise. "My lord, you are not mistaken. I am the mage."

I stare blankly for a moment before responding. "Do you take me for a fool?" I feel my mood changing. I do not have time for these games. Who does this woman think she is, to taunt me? It is common knowledge across Levanthria that a woman cannot wield magic strong enough to be classed as a mage.

"I do not taunt you, my lord. What would I achieve in such a heinous act?"

I stop myself from turning. Did this mysterious woman just read my thoughts? Did I speak aloud without realising?

She smiles seductively at me. "Yes, I did, and no, you didn't. There is a report."

I am confused by her words. Then a guard enters the hall and says, "Sir, there is a report."

The woman has earned five minutes of my time, but I do not trust her. I have never heard of a woman being connected to magic in such a way, and it will take a lot more for her to convince me otherwise.

"I am a seer, my lord. And I have had a vision that you will want to hear about."

22

VIREO

Necromancy is the darkest of magic that ever existed. It involves channelling the side effect of wielding magic into another body rather than your own. Transferring wounds from one person to another or even manipulating the dead to your will. It is even recorded that those with a powerful connection to magic are able to suck the life from another to extend their own. Such magic does not belong in this world and was banished far before the Benighted Thaumaturgist.

-Zaphire Etsom, alchemist, Temple of Eltera, 254 KR

Eventually, we come to a halt in the darkness and climb out of the cart, inspecting our surroundings. The forest is eery in its stillness, and only snatches of moonlight permeate the thick canopy above.

Now that we seem to be in relative safety, my companions take the opportunity to unleash their anger.

"You have damned us, Vireo!" Gillam hisses. "Our homes are gone. You know we can't return."

"We're alive, aren't we?" I fire back.

"We will be lucky to last a few days in here," Lek barks, eyeing the forest that surrounds us.

"We just have to make it through the night. We'll use the cart for shelter."

"We are here because of you!" Gillam removes a dagger from her side and moves with the speed and fury of a raging river in my direction. I do not move. If she strikes me down, at least this feeling will end. It is what I deserve.

Lek grabs her from behind at the last second and pulls her away from me, and her dagger only just misses my chest.

For a second, I think that Lek is on my side, but he shoves her away and crashes his boulder-like fist into my chest, sending me sprawling to the ground.

"I will stop her from killing you, but that doesn't mean I'm not angry with you." He leans down and grabs me by the scruff of my neck, dragging me to my feet as if I weigh nothing. He draws me towards his face. "You are a greedy fool, Vireo, with your blasted inability to abstain from things that do not belong to you."

I swat his hand away. "Allana was no man's possession," I snap at him, enraged that he would even suggest it. I take a swing at him. Allana may be dead, but I can still defend her honour.

Lek dodges my strike with ease, then slaps me to the ground once more. I land face-first into the mud, and he places his boot on my back. I am too resigned to bother struggling.

"You were happy enough to go along with my plan," I splutter into the mud, breathing in the damp earth.

In truth, I deserve whatever punishment Lek and Gillam may have for me. Because of me, Allana is dead, and

I will have to carry that for the rest of my life. I don't even try to get up. I just want to sink into the mud, to end this misery.

"It's only a matter of time before the beasts in this wretched place take us. Let's give him to them as bait, Lek. I'm taking my chances out there." Gillam re-sheathes her dagger and heads off towards an opening in the dense surroundings.

"Gillam, stop," I rasp, pushing myself into a crouch. Something has caught my eye.

"Don't tell me what to –" but Gillam is slammed to the ground by a hulking shadow. A wolfaire pins her to the floor, baring its teeth.

The horned wolf is huge, its matted grey fur standing on edge as it lets out a deep grumble.

"Get it off me!" She jams her gauntlet into the creature's mouth to prevent it from tearing her face off. The wolfaire snaps frantically, attempting to end Gillam's life.

Lek runs towards it and kicks it with all his might. The beast yelps and tumbles off Gillam, but it is quickly back on all fours and strikes again. Lek uses the shaft of his great axe to stop the beast from tearing into his flesh, but now it has the handle caught between its teeth.

I throw myself at the wolfaire, using my shoulder to knock it off balance, and the force is enough for it to let go of the axe. The three of us stand in a line, Gillam with her daggers, Lek with his axe, and me with one arrow in my hand. The wolfaire looks up, its bloodshot eyes wild with rage. A haunting howl leaves its mouth, and my blood runs cold. Wolfaires do not hunt on their own, and it is calling for its pack.

There is a rustle in the trees, and another three wolfaires appear behind the alpha male, each of them varying shades of brown. There is more movement behind us, and another three emerge, baring their teeth. We adapt our formation instinctively so that we are all back-to-back.

We do not stand a chance against this many.

I wait in anticipation as the wolfaires growl at us, unsure which one is going to strike first. They circle us, snapping erratically.

"They are starving!" Gillam points out, confirming my own thoughts on the matter.

The alpha snarls ferociously at us and I know it is only a matter of time before it makes its move. I brace myself for a painful death.

Something stirs, and another large wolfaire emerges, leaping out from the trees. Just as I ready myself for it to sink its teeth into my flesh, it turns, facing against the others.

"Is that – by the gods, it is! That's the wolfaire we released from the snare!" Lek's voice booms.

Before us stands the jet black wolfaire, its large, twisted horns pointed in the direction of the alpha. The growls and snarls filling the space around us are loud enough that I can barely hear my own breathing as my adrenaline spikes my senses.

Within a moment, all the wolfaires surrounding us bow their heads and begin to submit to the jet-black beast that stands in our defence.

"It's challenging the alpha!" Lek looks on in awe, as if excited at the prospect of the fight we are about to see.

Looking at the size of the two wolfaires, all I know is that I would not like to be in between the two of them. In an instant, the two monstrous beasts collide as they ram their heads against one another, each trying to best the other.

There is a flurry of white and black as they wrestle with each other in a heap on the floor. Then I hear a large yelp. The two beasts part, and the white wolfaire stands with its front paw raised. Blood drips on the ground in front of it. The black wolfaire continues to growl at our enemy until eventually the white alpha bows its head, turns, and disappears into the darkness.

"It's won, it will take its place as alpha," Lek says, releasing an uneasy laugh.

Gillam scowls. "Thank you for the commentary, but I know how this works."

The new alpha lets out a howl, and the others join. It is a haunting noise that would normally be the final auditory experience of any unlucky enough to find themselves in this situation. For some reason, however, I feel that we are now safe. The wolfaire has defended us, as if returning the favour for us rescuing it just a few days earlier. The new alpha turns and faces us momentarily before heading off into the darkness of the woods. The others follow.

We are still alive. For now.

23

VIREO

We use the cart for shelter. At night, one of us stands guard, but Lek's snoring resonates through the dense space like a wild bear, proving enough to ward off any potential beasts in the night. No more wolfaires appear. I do not feel tired; I feel nothing other than grief and guilt.

We have been in this wretched place for two days now, and we grow increasingly hungry. What little supplies we had with us are now gone, and the coin I had packed to start a new life with Allana has no value here.

I stir in my makeshift bed that is fashioned from branches and large canopy leaves. I have slept very little, if at all. Each time I close my eyes, all I see is the fatal shot that I took, Allana's bright green eyes dulling until the flame in them dies away. When I fall asleep, I am haunted by her cries and screams in the moments before I killed her. I deserve to be cursed by these nightmares for the rest of my life.

Sitting up, I see Gillam staring into the darkness, the small fire next to her dimming as the light from the sun forces its way in between the surrounding trees. I can hear various crows and chirps from the birds above us, but now and then, I am certain I catch the distant growls and roars of the beasts that live deeper within the forest – a constant reminder of the dangers that lurk around us.

Neither Gillam or Lek have spoken much to me in the last forty-eight hours, and I am surprised that Gillam has not chosen to end me while I sleep.

Lek chokes in his sleep, startling himself awake.

I position myself closer to the small campfire to gather what warmth I can from it before it extinguishes. Crackling embers drift from the fire, drawing my gaze. I can feel myself becoming lost as I stare into the flames.

"What is left of the supplies?" Lek asks, stretching his arms and letting out an enormous yawn.

"There's nothing left," says Gillam. "We need to hunt, otherwise we won't last long."

"Hunt *what*?" I snap a twig and toss it into the flames. "I am pretty sure we are on the menu for most of the creatures that inhabit this place, not the other way around." I agree that we need food, but hunting in this place would likely bring an end to us, if the stories we all grew up with are to be believed.

"Shall we all just sit around and wait for the fate that you've consigned us to?" Lek growls, walking over to pick his great axe up from the back of the cart. He heads off into the trees, even though he does not know where they will take us.

"You cannot go by yourself, Lek." I grab my sword and follow, but I keep my distance so that he can't reach me with his weapon.

"I'll stay and guard the horses," Gillam grumbles.

With this, Lek and I begin our journey through the

forest on the hunt for some food. It is an eerie place with differing shapes of trees, some small, some the largest I have ever seen. The light pushes its way through the canopy from time to time, giving the smallest reprieve and natural warmth from the sun. The earthy pine smell in the air emits a refreshing fragrance – a relief, compared to the squalor of the slums.

We walk for what feels like hours with no sign of game. Why does the forest tease us so? We can hear the chirping birds above us, the odd rustling of leaves; we just cannot see anything, and this keeps us both on edge. We could find ourselves set upon at any moment, so we must stay alert and ready to strike.

Using my sword, I hack against the large leaves and branches in front of me. I see more natural light ahead, then I notice the trees thinning. We have reached the outer edge of the forest. Pushing our way through the last of the thicket, we step out from the trees, and I breathe a sigh of relief. In an instant, I feel safer. But I know there is likely a huge bounty on our heads, and even if we were to head to a new town, our safety would not last long.

"I never thought I would say it, but I think we are safer in the forest. For now, anyway." Raising my head, I soak up the sun as it casts its warmth down on us.

"That is about the only thing I have to agree with you on." This is the most Lek has spoken to me since we left Gillam to hunt. I don't blame him. This situation is my fault in its entirety. My ego led us on this path. My desire to take whatever I want has nearly cost us our lives, and Allana has paid for it with hers.

"What now?" Lek parks his giant frame against a large rock beside us. "We can't just wander around aimlessly, Vireo, we will not last much longer."

I could point out that Lek is the one who decided to wander away from camp, into the unknown depths of the forest, but I hold my tongue. There is a time and a place for reprimands, and now is not the moment. Not unless I wish to be pummelled into the ground once again. My lip has only just stopped throbbing from his last blow.

Instead, I say, "Let's leave some traps and come back to them in the morning."

Lek nods in resentful agreement. Then something beyond him in the distance catches my eye, and an idea sparks to life.

"Lek." I point behind him. "Looks like a caravan."

Lek's bearded face erupts with a smile when he understands the opportunity. "They must use this route as a shortcut. Explains the guards."

Lek is right; guards trot on horseback on either side of the passenger wagon, protecting whoever is inside. Behind this is another supply cart of some sort.

"Most likely a nobleman." I think out loud. "Quick – to the trees." We scurry behind the large trees on the outer edge of the forest and wait for the cart to draw closer. The guards on horseback have the upper hand, but I'm sure if we can startle the horses, we may just about get away with this.

We lie in wait as the caravan approaches. Normally prior to a fight, I would feel a surge of invigorating adrenaline. But right now, I feel nothing. The only thing keeping me going is a need to get some food for Lek and Gillam, who have risked their lives for me.

Within a few minutes, I can hear the horses trotting along and the wheels of the carriage grinding against the dirt track. For encouragement, I reach into my satchel and pull out Allana's emerald hood, breathing in her scent.

Then I place the hood over my head to hide my identity, the torn cloak draping down my back.

No doubt there will be posters of my face everywhere. We need to play the right hand to get one over the guards. I take a deep breath before nodding at Lek, and I stagger out from the trees into the path of the cart.

"Whoa!" The man steering the carriage pulls on the reins and the caravan comes to an abrupt stop. "What are you doing?" He demands, his balding head wet with the sweat from the heat. He is of average build and wears the colours of the noble house he works for; purple and black diagonal stripes decorate both his tunic and the flag attached to the top of the carriage.

"I beg pardon, sir. I have been lost for days," I say, putting a southern accent on and stuttering with my words.

"What is going on out there?" a well-spoken voice calls from inside the carriage.

"Just a man claiming to be lost, sire," one guard calls back from atop his black horse. He is wearing a helmet, but his face is not protected, and I can see his red moustache with hints of grey, which suggest he is an older man and may be easier to take down. I still have relative youth on my side.

"Just move him out of the way. I do not have time or interest in helping common folk," the voice calls back, frustration apparent in his tone.

With this, the second guard, who rides a grey horse, rushes around me to usher me out of the way. Horses are often used for crowd control because they instil fear and panic amongst men with the threat of being trampled, but I do not know fear. I stand my ground and the horse bucks up. The guard just barely manages to stay on his horse.

I place my hands up in the air and feign cowering. "I mean no harm, sir. All I ask is for a lift to the nearest town. I can sit on the cart at the back, I won't be no bother."

"Except you already are." The guard with the red moustache grits his teeth and kicks me to the ground.

"What is taking so long?" The voice from inside bellows out. "Deal with whoever is causing this delay. He may not ride with us, but I suggest you put him out of his misery."

The younger guard drops from his horse and unsheathes his sword. His mistake; he has now lost his high ground. As he steps towards me, I remove my sword and block his blade when he attempts to bring it down on me. I drop the act and stand taller than the humped impression I was giving. I swing my sword to his right and he parries it. The older and more experienced guard has his sword ready, but remains on his horse, and I expect a strike from above.

From the trees, Lek roars, his great axe fixed in both his hands as he builds up momentum. For someone with such a hulking frame, he can certainly move fast. Like a battering ram, he charges into the side of the horse, causing it to buck and dismount the older soldier. As I watch this, I almost let the younger guard catch me by surprise, but I step back and parry his attack.

Two more horsemen – one from the carriage and one from the cart at the rear – join the fight, making it four against two. Each of them has their swords drawn, but I can tell by their hesitance that they are not experienced fighters. We will be able to use this to our advantage.

The young guard swings again and again, and I parry each blow with ease, studying his movements. Then he takes a wild lunge at me. I step to the side, and the momentum of his swing spins him on the spot. I do not have the intention of ending this man's life, so I take the opportunity and wrap my arm around him, choking him out until he falls. I glance across to Lek, who has rendered the older guard unconscious; he lies sprawled out on the floor.

We turn to face the two horsemen, who are both shakily pointing their swords at us, but they are trembling so badly that they can barely keep hold of their weapons.

"We do not wish to harm you," I tell them. "We are in need of supplies, and as if by divine intervention, you have stumbled across our paths. May I make a suggestion? No blood needs to be spilled. Take your carriage and continue to wherever it is you are heading. We will take the cart."

"Insolence! Kill them now!" the voice shrieks from inside.

Lek and I are ready. With any luck, the remaining men will see sense. They do, and both jump onto the carriage. Lek picks up the moustached guard and lays him over his horse's saddle. I do the same with the younger guard.

"I said kill them!" the voice shouts again.

I grow tired of the man, so I head to the window and open the side door. In front of me sits an oversized, pompous nobleman with an abundance of fruit and wine around him.

"We will be taking that." As I lean forward, the fat nobleman attempts to lash me with his hand. I drive my fist into his face. Hoping that will shut him up for the moment, I grab what fruit I can, and the bottle of wine that sits beside him.

Lek slaps the horses' rears, and they gallop off with the guards unconsciously riding them. The horsemen gee their stallions, and the carriage sets off away from us, leaving the cart.

"Well, that went well." I smile at Lek. "For a moment I didn't think you were going to come out and help me."

"I nearly didn't," he says, his face expressionless.

I pull back the cloth that covers contents of the abandoned cart, and our faces light up. It is filled with fruit, vegetables, and a medium-sized pig. My stomach churns. The sight of so much food is a welcome sensation. Never have red apples appeared so bright or carrots so delectable. Even the swedes make our mouths water. There is enough food to last us half a moon.

"There's wine!" Lek rejoices.

"We'll take the fruit and vegetables. Leave the pig," I say.

"Are you mad?"

"Leave it. I don't want it to attract the wolfaires to our camp. I'd rather they feast on it and not on us."

In the end, we take the pig. Just in case.

24

JAREB

Half a moon cycle has passed since Allana's death and my first meeting with Morgana. The seer, having proven her ability to predict the immediate future, tells me she has had a vision.

This vision came to her in her dreams, but it was clear as day; it showed a battle in the city walls of Askela. The people taking over and overthrowing my rule, and my death at the hands of a man in a green hood. Morgana also says that Jordell's work will bear fruit. When these things will come to pass, she cannot say.

Around twenty men and women of varying ages await me in the courtyard. The sound of my footsteps draws an echo off the stones – such is the silence that befalls the courtyard upon my arrival. Today, I must pass judgement on those who have committed crimes against the crown, or have not paid their taxes.

Morgana waits for me at the bottom of the staircase. She wears a black dress today, with a plunging V at the front that reveals her form. Her red hair shines with the sun overhead, and she casts a smile at me. I nod to her in greeting.

"My lord." Her soft voice soothes me, keeping my impending headache at bay.

I hold out my hand, which she takes, and we walk to a large, gilded chair that has been set out for me. I used to hate these meetings, but since Morgana's arrival, my decision-making has felt decidedly easier.

Sitting back in the chair, I feel the comfort of the cushioned seat and rest my hands on the arms of the dark wood.

"Shall we begin?" I wave at Codrin to bring over the first of the prisoners. Codrin's strong build is clear beneath his chain mail. He wears a tunic over his armour, which bears the yellow and white of his family's crest. His long black hair is tied back from his face, revealing his pointed ears, which match his sharp nose and thin face. It is rare to see such a brute with links to elven ancestry.

Codrin escorts a young man before me, his clothes tattered and ripped, most likely from his arrest. He has blonde hair, and I cannot see the colour of his eyes because of the swelling.

"Did he put up a fight when arrested?" I question.

"Indeed, my lord. This man injured two guards while they arrested him for stealing rice from the market."

"What is your defence?" I ask.

"Please, my lord, I steal only to provide for my family," the man stutters.

My head throbs enough for me to bring my hands to my temple. My eyes sting from the sun bearing down on me. "Yet you see fit to injure two of my men to avoid arrest?" I turn to Morgana, who leans down to my ear. The sweet smell of flowers overcomes me from the perfume that she wears. The dull ache within my head lessens as she moves closer to me.

"He tells the truth," she whispers. "His family starves and is reliant on him. Show some mercy and he can still contribute to the crown. I can test my magic on him."

"For the crime of theft, I declare one lashing. For the crime of injuring two of my guards, an additional two lashings," I say for all to hear. "For each guard injured." I know that five lashings might cut deep to the bone, but I need to set an example for others.

"Please, no! Have mercy!" the man begs and pleads as two of Codrin's men drag the offender to a post that stands to the right of me. They wrap his arms around it and bind his hands. One guard pulls out a small knife and cuts the back of the prisoner's already-tattered top to reveal his back.

Codrin removes the coiled whip from his belt and lets it unfurl across the floor. He is someone who can only be described as torturous for his masterful ability to inflict punishment.

He waves the whip slowly, then he flicks it forward. The end contacts the man's flesh. He holds in his scream well for the first lashing, but by the third, he lets out a guttural cry. Those that stand in wait for their crimes to be heard gasp and avert their eyes.

Flesh parts from the man's body with each blow, and when the final lashing strikes, blood splatters on the ground around him.

"*Throw him in the dungeon!*" the voice hisses in the centre of my mind, causing me to wince. "*Show them what happens if they defy the crown. There is work the seer can do. Let her test her magic on him.*" Each word stabs at my eyes. The voice sounds as if it is in agony, the shrill words causing the skin on my arms to run cold.

I wave him away. "Take him to the dungeon." I feel myself staring vacantly as I speak.

"Thank you, my lord," Morgana soothes. Again, the pain in my head subsides.

The man's screaming becomes more and more muffled as he is dragged away.

Today is going to be a long day.

"*Well done,*" the voice takes over once more. "*The people will listen. People will do what you wish of them if they see you will not take insolence lightly.*"

I slowly nod in agreement but quickly adjust myself before others notice.

"Codrin!" I shout. "How many of these people are here for non-payment of taxes?"

"Fifteen, my lord."

I need to ensure the people of Askela keep on top of their payments to the crown. I'll show them what happen to those who do not.

"One lashing to each person who stands here today for non-payment of taxes. Then throw them back out through the gates."

Codrin nods. "What about the other four?"

"What are their crimes?"

"Theft, and one wench spat at a guard."

"One lashing each and then into the dungeon. Morgana needs to perfect her magic."

"*They will listen.*" The voice fades out in my mind, and I feel my headache subsiding again.

I will not be defied.

25

JAREB

T o have magic coursing through your veins is not a gift, it is a curse placed by the gods. The side effects for those that use magic is heinous. This includes wrinkled and worn skin, skin as cold as ice, and pain and agony after wielding magical spells. What's worse, the more you use, the more the addiction takes you. The more you use the more your body becomes worn and broken, until the mind ends up in a state where it does not know what is real and what is madness.

  -Zaphire Etsom, alchemist, Temple of Eltera, 254 KR

Having taken care of the morning's proceedings, I now sit at the large oak table eating chicken that has been prepared for me. The light shines in through the large stained-glass window, which has a colourful image of the king sitting atop his white stallion. His sword in one hand, his shield bearing the crest of a lion in the other.

"Lord Jareb, Jordell requests an audience with you." The guard's words snap me from my thoughts. I nod at him to allow Jordell in.

With any luck, he will have transcribed that blasted spell book. Given the time he has had it now, I do expect the process to be well under way.

Jordell enters, looking dishevelled. I notice a beard is forming, and he looks even worse than what I have become accustomed to.

"How is that spell book coming along, Jordell?" No use in wasting time.

"I am making some progress, but not as much as I had hoped. I've been busy preparing healing salves for those who have received lashes," he says. His eyes shine with quiet defiance.

"Is that a criticism of me, Jordell?"

"I dare not criticise you. However, I cannot turn my back on the people of Askela that need me. People are falling on even harder times of late, with the increase in taxes and the plague."

"THEN I SUGGEST YOU FOCUS ON THAT SPELL BOOK!" I roar as I slam my fist into the table so hard that my tankard falls over, spilling my water. "Did you care to think that if you cracked this book, you might conjure magic to aid you in your quest to fix people?" My frustration at the lack of development grows. "I am to assume that you have magical abilities."

"Yes, I mean only a little. I use my ability in my potions," Jordell stammers.

"Perhaps you require the right motivation, Jordell." I take a blood red apple from the table and bite into it. The crunch itself is satisfying, but what follows is an explosion of flavour. "Those that were lashed and released earlier today for crimes against the crown, the ones who appear to be distracting you . . . For every day that spell book is not transcribed, I shall call one person back and I will hold them in the dungeon for Morgana to experiment on."

The colour drains from Jordell's face until his skin becomes a pale grey, and his dark eyes dart around the room. I wonder if the man is going to faint on me.

"Jareb, she cannot be trusted. Women should not be able to wield any magic. It is not natural." He is struggling to string his words together.

"Do not talk ill of Morgana, Jordell. She has been of great service to me, and to the crown."

"Jareb, she claims to be a seer, but visions can be manipulated. What if she is doing this with you?" he continues, and my temper flares.

"Is there an issue, my lord?" Morgana appears behind Jordell, and he looks like he's going to shrink into the ground. Her words are delicate, like soft cotton.

I laugh to myself at Jordell's discomfort. "Jordell was just telling me I ought to be careful around you, Morgana. Women and magic or something, wasn't it?" I divert my attention back to Jordell. I enjoy watching him squirm. Since Allana's betrayal, it is only Morgana who has offered me any form of support. I felt that I would never trust another woman again, but she stepped in straight away and filled the void left behind.

"I wouldn't worry, my lord. He had a low opinion of me when I was part of the Great Temple in Yefral." She walks past him, her hourglass figure slowly circling him like an animal ready to strike its prey.

"Not – not just me," Jordell says, giving me the impression he does not like confrontation. Something else doesn't sit right. There is more that has happened here between these two. "There were rumours, rumours of dark magic. It is why you were cast out."

Morgana feigns shock in a playful manner, all the while continuing to circle him like a coiled viper. Then it dawns on me. Jordell is intimidated by her. He fears her. A mere woman who has the ability to wield magic.

"Magic is magic, Jordell. Do you think in war that the winning side will care what form is used? All that matters is that the tides of war move in our favour." I stand from the table, having finished my lunch, and place my hands behind my back while I talk.

"And many will die in the process of this dark magic. Not just on the battlefield," Jordell says, stiffening. He seems to be regaining composure.

"If that is what it takes, then so be it," I scoff. "If you do not wish for the dark magic to be developed, it is in your power. All you need to do is transcribe that book!"

Morgana stops circling and speaks softly into Jordell's ear. "I'd hurry if I were you. Your time lessens, and I am in need of more men and women to test my magic on."

Jordell shuffles back the look of shock on his face and makes for the exit without another word.

26
VIREO

It takes us most of the day of hacking through underbrush to get the cart back to camp. When we arrived, Gillam cracks a smile for the first time in days.

My shoulders ache deeply. I would use all the coin I have for a deep massage right now. I have been on edge all day, half-expecting the creatures we can hear in the distance to strike. All the while, Lek swore we were being stalked by something throughout our journey, and the odd rustle in the bushes appeared to support his theory.

"How on earth?" Gillam's jaw is agape at the feat we have achieved. "Where did you find a bloody cart in here?"

Lek roared with laughter. "You would not believe our luck. There we were at the edge of the forest when a caravan just happened to pass us by, like a gift from the gods."

"And what of the men whom that cart belonged to?" Gillam folds her arms.

I smile. "We sent them on their way."

"Shame. I'm sure their carcasses would have kept the beasties away from us for a time," Gillam says, smirking.

Lek pulls an apple out of a sack and crunches into it. "Those men did no wrong, and they didn't deserve to lose their lives."

"I don't know, Lek. That lord tried my patience – and he tried to have me killed."

"As a consequence of our actions," Lek says, ever the reasonable one. For a man so ferocious in battle, he is such a gentle giant when not on the battlefield. "That lord's ill will was no different than the thoughts that have been circling my head about you these last few days."

Maybe he is not such a gentle soul after all. Maybe my own actions have corrupted him to this point. I can't help but let out a nervous laugh as I remove Allana's hood.

"And the point of that is . . . ?" Gillam asks, nodding toward the emerald cloak.

"He says it's to hide his face. The fool won't admit that he wears it because it was her ladyship's," Lek says.

I feel a rush of anger and draw my sword. "Do not speak ill of Allana," I threaten. Lek raises his hands in defeat and shrugs, laughing at me. After a moment, I laugh, too. I cannot believe I have just drawn my sword on Lek after the beating he gave me when we first arrived here. I re-sheathe my sword and offer my hand as an apology, which Lek thankfully accepts.

Gillam rolls her eyes at us and turns her attention to the cart of supplies. "What have we got then?" Her eyes light up as she reaches in and grabs hold of two bottles of red wine. "Gentlemen, can I interest you in a tipple?"

That is just like Gillam to avoid the food and focus on the wine. No wonder why she is so thin and agile. Lek, on the other hand, is salivating at the sight of all the luscious colours of the fruits and vegetables. I fear for a moment that Lek is about to dive in and eat the lot, but he appears to control his urges.

"We need to make these supplies last. We need to survive in this forest for as long as we can. I dread to think about the bounty that is on our heads outside of our ever-green home."

"I cannot survive on paltry rations," Lek proclaims, "look at the size of me!" It's the most animated I've seen him all day.

"Maybe you could live off the wildlife growing in that beard of yours?" Gillam says before removing the cork from the wine bottle with her teeth. The proceeding *pop* is most satisfying to the ears. She places the bottle to her lips and takes in a glug. "Now that is the sweetest thing I have ever tasted." She passes the bottle to Lek, who follows suit. This appears to soothe him momentarily, and he continues to chug at the bottle like suckling babe.

"Steady on, old boy." Gillam grabs the bottle before he necks it in its entirety. After I take moment to indulge – relishing the warmth from the alcohol as it lines my throat, and savouring the taste of wild berries – it's time to get serious.

"If we are to survive out here, we need to put the vegetables to good use." I unload a crate of potatoes. Walking to an open patch of ground at the edge of our makeshift camp, I drop to my knees, placing the box beside me. I then dig a hole with my hands before lining up some potatoes inside the box and covering the soil over them.

"Great, so we're farmers now?" Gillam's tone oozes sarcasm. "How long do you expect us to be out here?"

Lek has started chopping vegetables for stew. "For the foreseeable," he says, answering for me. "We need to be prepared to wait this out in the long term." He throws some kindling on the campfire. "Vireo speaks sense, Gillam."

I pat down the soil and take the rest of the crate of vegetables to Lek, who has fashioned his chest plate into a makeshift pan.

"And the pig?" Gillam asks. "Do you plan on planting that, too?"

"Don't be so ridiculous." I drag the pig to the edge of the cart, grabbing hold of its trotters, the weight of it far too much for me to lift by myself. "Here, give me a hand."

Gillam reluctantly helps me lift the pig out of the back and I direct us into the trees outside of our camp. "What are we doing, Vireo?"

"Feeding the starving wolfaires," I say. "The gods only know why, but I think they are the only thing stopping us from becoming a meal for whatever else is out there."

"And how do you expect to appease these wolfaires?" Gillam asks, unconvinced.

We drop the pig in front of a cluster of older trees, their impressive trunks twisting and winding around one another. "Why, we will continue to rob the carts that travel past the outskirts of the forest, of course."

We might just survive this.

27
VIREO

We all agree to the food rationing plan, but we decide there is no point in rationing the wine, so we merrily make our way through eight of the fifteen bottles. This seems to put Lek and Gillam in better spirits, but I drink to dull my mind, hoping that when I eventually pass out, I might actually find some solace in sleep.

For now, sleep will have to wait; it's my turn to stand guard on the edge of the camp. The other two are out cold. Gillam slumbers on the bed of leaves, and Lek sits upright against the cart. We tipped it on its side and fashioned a roof by tying the cover sheet over it. He sits with his head tilted back, and his giant hand is clenched so tightly around a bottle of wine that I wonder if it has fused to the glass.

The more I drink, the more the forest appears to dance around me. It is at night when this place truly comes alive, and for now my plan is to stand guard, drink, and watch the night breathe life into the forest.

Numb grief, hunger, and fear had blinded me to our surroundings the first few nights. But now I sip my wine and study the glowing mushrooms and night flowers that illuminate the forest around me with the most vibrant, luminous colours. Green, blue, and yellow areas of the forest radiate as the lights fade away in this place. I cannot tell if the fungus that populates the trees is pulsating, or if my eyes are playing tricks on me because of the wine.

I fall into a trance where I can feel each of my heartbeats. I feel around my body and the surrounding lights dim at the same time, as though we are connected.

I glance down at the bottle in my hand which is nearly empty, and take in another glug, my vision becoming increasingly blurred with each mouthful. The forest is a welcome distraction from thoughts of Allana, the thoughts of the life we should have been living now, with our child growing inside of her.

For a moment, it appears as if there are streams of light forming all around me. I close my eyes and I can feel myself swaying, as though taken by a gentle breeze as the zig-zagging lights penetrate my eyelids. I wonder what they are – insects, bound to the forest? I've never experienced anything like it.

Then the whispers reach me.

"Vireo," a gentle voices murmurs in my ears, and I open my eyes with haste.

"Who goes there? Show yourself." I stagger up, ready for a fight.

"Allana," another whisper blows over my shoulder, and I spin around.

"Temptation," another whisper billows past me – this one I feel on the shoulder, as if something has just pushed me.

The next whisper calls, "Greed," and I feel another caress.

"Change," a last wisp of air drifts into my ear, and a larger blow to my chest is strong enough to make me stumble. My heel hits against something and I fall for what feels like an eternity, the world slowing around me. For a moment I pray for the earth and leaves around me to engulf me in their embrace – for all this to end – and I hit the forest floor, a slight pain rising in the back of my head. As I stare up at the canopy of leaves above, the lights continue to dart about me and my mind drifts away from me.

Then everything goes black, and I slip into unconsciousness.

I blink my eyes to acclimate to the daylight that greets me. Did I fall asleep while on watch? I have a vague recollection of the night before – visions of swirling lights and whispers from the trees.

A sharp pain pierces the back of my head and I bring my hand up to check for an injury. I can feel a lump, but when I remove my hand, there is no blood. I must have drunk too much.

Letting out a sigh, I close my eyes against the bright morning sun. I wonder if I can get away with going back to sleep, but then I think how Gillam and Lek would respond if they were to catch me compromising their safety.

I hear crunching of branches and leaves underfoot and I sit bolt upright, canvassing my surroundings.

A boy stands at the rear of the stolen cart, and appears to be helping himself to our supplies. His clothes are filthy and torn, and his blonde, unkempt hair is darkened and matted with dirt. He is thin, most likely from malnourishment. I can see he is trying to be quiet, but he does not share Gillam's skill of stealth.

The boy freezes in his tracks like a startled deer when he sees me, a large red apple in his hand. What little colour he had in his face drains.

"Please, sir, show kindness," he squeaks.

"When you are taking our supplies?" My head is throbbing, and I do not take kindly to being woken like this. I climb to my feet and brush dirt and leaves from my tunic.

The boy draws a sword, and I am taken by the boy's belief that he could fell me. I can't help but laugh.

"And what do you suppose you are going to do with that, boy?"

"Whatever I need to," he fires back. This boy has some guts. He may be stupid, but he has guts.

"Just a moment ago you asked for kindness, and now you draw your sword on me? What do you think is the likely outcome of this?" My head continues to throb. "I am not in the mood for this."

"Nor am I, Vireo." The boy knows my name, and this piques my interest.

He answers my next question before I can ask it. "There is a bounty on your head. One hundred coins. I could just bring the guards here. This forest must not be as dangerous as everyone is led to believe if you've been able to survive."

"That wouldn't be wise. A hundred coins, though? I would turn me in for that."

"What the blasts is all this noise! Vireo, who are you talking to?" Lek roars. He sees the boy with his sword pointed in my direction and scrambles to his feet, something that takes longer than most men because of his size "Gillam!"

He kicks Gillam and startles her awake. She is nowhere near as alert as she normally is, which isn't a surprise; she drank enough wine to sink three men last night. "What is going on?" She jumps to her feet, taking in the situation.

"I count it three against one, boy. You may want to rethink your strategy."

"Tie him up!" Gillam demands.

Lek tosses me my sword, and I unsheathe it, pointing my blade at our mysterious guest. "Stand down, I can manage this."

Lek and Gillam sigh, clearly disappointed at only being able to spectate this fight.

"Are you sure you want to do this?"

"Let me leave with what I carry, and I will bring no harm or threats," the boy suggests.

"It's a little late for that now, isn't it?" I lunge forward with my blade and strike from above. To my surprise, the boy parries it away – but he does look as if he is ready to drop his sword. He's still too small to wield a weapon with one arm. He realises this and drops the fruits, wrapping both hands around the hilt of his sword, adopting an offensive stance, which surprises me.

He steps forward and strikes. I knock his blade away but he uses his momentum to take a huge swing at me, and I'm forced to step back so that I do not lose my head. Pressing forward, I slash my sword sideways. The boy blocks this away and spins, aiming another blow. I raise my sword in time, but I need to use both hands to ensure my blade is not pushed into me.

"Could it be that Vireo is about to be bested by a boy?" Lek bellows as he laughs. "Saves us doing the job."

I am impressed by the boy's skills, and can't help but think that he has received formal training. There is no way he could fight like this at such a young age simply by chance.

"How is it you have become so well accustomed to a blade?" I ask him as we dance around one another.

The boy takes another swipe, which I block again. "I was a squire!" He swings towards me multiple times, which I parry before he raises his sword high above him.

Sensing my opportunity, I drop to the floor and sweep kick his legs from underneath him. The boy loses his footing and, with the weight of his sword above his head, fall backwards into the back of the stolen cart.

I grab a fistful of his clothes and pull him close. His green eyes stare back at me, unflinching and determined. I toss him to the ground before stretching out my sword to his throat. He continues to stare up at me from the ground, his teeth clenched.

"Do you yield?"

28

JAREB

The dungeon is a wretched place. Darkness and the smell of decay mix with the screams and cries of the men and women that find themselves here. If they had only done their part to fight against the enemy, they would not be here.

A stinging pain joined by a high-pitched noise pierces my mind. My headache torments me.

The air in the corridor feels wet, and the sound of dripping water echoes as I make my way down the black tunnel. The only reprieve of light is the burning torch I hold out in front of me. Black stone shines on either side of me, displaying gaps from crumbling mortar, and dark green mould and moss blankets vast sections of the wall.

A scream from a man startles me, coming from nearby. I have not been down here for years, but now I've come to see what Morgana does down here. The screams get louder and louder, until they suddenly stop, which sends a shiver down my spine. Still, needs must if we are to gain the advantage and wield powerful magic for the first time in a millennium.

I continue down the winding corridors until I see a glow of amber light just ahead. When I step inside, I am not prepared for what I see.

There are two racks lined up. One holds the man I had Codrin lash many times. His face is gaunt and withdrawn, his eyes sunken and dark. His hands are chained above him, and his head is slumped forward, body limp. Streaks of dirt and blood decorate his exposed torso, but I see his chest rising slowly, meaning that for now, he remains alive and still of use for our cause. Opposite him, a woman lies on top of an old wooden table, leather straps binding her in place. Her skin bulges around them, red from the swelling. Her eyes are filled with tears. Her cries, however, are silent.

"My lord, what brings you here?" Morgana's soft voice eases any discomfort that I am feeling about the sight before me. The shrill noise that is etched into my mind subsides at her presence. She sits at her desk, and a candle flickers in front of her, illuminating the parchment on which she has been writing. "I am just scribing my findings so far." She speaks as though she has read my mind once more, appearing to know the answers to my unasked questions.

"I am here to see what you have been doing down here to further your magic, but you already knew that."

Morgana's cheeks dimple as she laughs gently. Even in this darkness, she radiates beauty and brings light to this place. She slides her chair back which scrapes against the stone floor, and approaches the woman. She strokes her hand delicately up the woman's arm, who shakes and tries to pull away, to no avail. Morgana continues up the woman's arm until she reaches her face, wiping her tears away with the back of her hand.

"Now, child. Show bravery in front of our lord. You have

been most helpful in this crusade." Morgana directs her gaze at me, still smiling. I cannot help but find her alluring. "Care for a demonstration, my lord?"

I nod and steady my nerves as Morgana picks up a small dagger from the table next to the woman.

"Please don't," the woman sobs.

"Morgana? What is it you do?" I find the sight of her with a blade in hand unnerving. Have we gone too far in our quest to turn the tides of war in our favour? Have we pushed beyond the possibility of redeeming our souls?

Morgana takes the blade and runs the tip down the woman's arm, whose screams instantly echo throughout the chamber. My heart races and I begin to tremble. The blade slices through the woman's skin like paper, leaving a large gash running down the length of her left forearm. Blood pulsates from her arm and pool underneath her. Morgana places one of her hands over the bleeding arm and closes her eyes.

"*Ashtar clelum sinta tralus*," she chants over and over. The woman continues to bleed, something which I presume cannot go on for much longer. Morgana raises her free right hand and aims her open palm towards the other prisoner. "*Ashtar clelum sinta tralus*." She continues her chant until her hands glow red, a black energy forming in the centre. The magical glow is faint, but it is there.

The sight is breath-taking. I have never seen real magic, and the hairs on my arms stand on edge as my eyes widen at the marvel that is unfolding before me. The glow is enchanting, and I find myself drawn more and more to the unnatural light that Morgana wears like a pair of gloves.

The man in chains awakens.

"Please not again, no, no, no!" He shouts as soon as he

gains consciousness, and I know that this is not the first time he has experienced this.

"*Ashtar clelum sinta tralus.*" The strain of the magic shows on Morgana's body. Her veins bulge and her muscles tighten, but she does not stop. Her hair blows around her, making her look like a mythical creature rather than a human.

"Stop, please, I beg you." The man's words rise into a scream of agony and anguish as he convulses. My attention is drawn to his forearm, where a large gash rips through his skin. I glance at the woman and the cut on her arm disappears. Somehow Morgana is transferring the wound from one to the other. This is dark magic.

Morgana's eyes bulge but she continues the chant. As the woman's screams fade, the man's grow louder before the wound on the woman's arm disappears in its entirety. Then, Morgana breaks her spell, and her hands stop glowing. She stumbles backwards, looking faint. I reach her just in time, catching her in my arms. I notice the smell of almonds as I stand in her proximity. I welcome the reprieve from the odious fragrances that cling to this place.

She trembles in my arms. This magic has taken its toll on her, and I can see why. "Are you ok?" I ask with bated breath.

"We are," she answers.

The female prisoner appears somewhat calmer than she did a few moments ago. The screams of the man have also dulled, and he is no longer moving. I escort Morgana to her chair before tentatively moving towards him. An eery silence has replaced his screams of anguish and fear, and now the only sound is dripping blood that splashes against the wet stone floor. As I get closer to him, I notice that just in the past few minutes, his hair has greyed and his skin appears more weathered. His breathing has stopped.

I glance at Morgana. "He's dead."

"He has proved very useful, my lord. My magic is getting stronger each time I use it."

"But at what price? A life every time? To transfer a wound?"

Morgana purses her thin red lips. "My lord, I have practiced this multiple times with him. If we are going to achieve our goal, we need to make sacrifices." She grabs a cup from her desk and takes a drink of water, her hand trembling enough to make me feel she may drop it on the floor.

"I can see the toll this is taking on you."

"But imagine your forces when we can transfer our soldiers' open wounds to our enemies, and take their life forces to replenish ours. Your soldiers would be unstoppable. We just need Jordell to finish transcribing the book."

"I'm sure his efforts will bear fruit soon."

Morgana lifts the quill on her table and scribbles her findings on the parchment, and I turn to leave.

And there Jordell stands, the spell book gripped tightly against his chest. His face is pale and twisted with horror at the sight before him.

I realise he must have seen the entire thing.

29
JAREB

It is rumoured there are three witches to the north, living in isolation in the Pendaran Hills. The villagers blame them for this year's poor crops. As the people of the villagers become more agitated, it is only a matter of time before they march on their home and confront them.

-Goran Sien, written report to Jareb, KR 260 KR

The alchemist stumbles backwards.

"Jordell!" I yell as he spins on his heel and rushes in the opposite direction, his feet splashing on the sodden stone ground.

"Listen to me! This is something we must do if we are to end this war," I call out, following him. When he glances back, the fear is clear in his expression.

"*Stop him.*" The voice hisses in my mind, a piercing pain engulfing my eyes like a red-hot poker. "*If he tells of our experiments, the people of this city will burn the castle to the ground.*"

"Guards!" My words echo down the dank corridor like a pebble skipping on water. "Fetch Jordell back to me!"

Two guards farther down the corridor follow Jordell, who has now picked up pace as he reaches a bend in the halls. As my words echo towards him, he looks back before setting off, running out of sight.

"God's blazing!" I curse as I set off at pace myself, a sudden sense of urgency overcoming me. Icy breath rushes from my mouth as I make my way after the healer, my footsteps sloshing through the dampness on the floor. The armour of my guards jangles loudly as they make chase down the hall.

When I reach the bottom of the winding pits, I see no one ahead of me—just the different doorways to dungeons that line the walls, the gateways to prisoners' personal hells. I hear the guards shouting out for Jordell to stop, and the sound of them unsheathing their blades reverberates off the stone walls. A flash of light fills my surroundings and I shield my eyes with my forearm, the light imprinting on the backs of my eyelids.

I hear groans coming from the other side of the hallway, and when I reach the end, I discover the two guards sprawled across the floor. One looks unconscious, the other wide-eyed.

"What happened? Where is Jordell?" I demand.

"Magic, sire. He – he used magic on us." The guard looks bewildered, his face raw with shock.

I continue my pursuit, gritting my teeth. Evidently, Jordell has made plenty of progress on the book.

If he hadn't just witnessed Morgana's little performance, he might have wilfully handed over the blasted information that I so desperately need.

Approaching the stairs to the exit, I skip them two at a

time, and I can only pray that I catch up to Jordell before it is too late.

The backs of my legs are burning by the time I reach the top step, and my heart thunders in my chest. Jordell is a bigger, slower man than me, so at this pace it is only a matter of time before I catch up.

When the courtyard comes into view, I see Jordell hurrying for his white horse, which waits by the gates.

"Jordell!" He is losing his pace and I am gaining ground on him.

Within a few moments, I catch up to him, his horse just a few metres away. I lunge forward, tackling him to the ground. The air pushes out of my lungs as we smash into the cobbled floor and skid to a stop. Jordell scrambles to his feet.

"Stop running! It is pointless." I clench my jaw almost as tightly as my fist.

"You condone dark magic, Jareb!" Jordell cries, reaching for the reins of his horse. "I cannot play a part in this."

"Jordell, listen to me. You need to stop." I snatch his trailing wrist and pull him backwards.

A soft glow emits from Jordell's hand and before I have time to think, I find myself thrown backwards by an unnatural force. The feeling of magic hitting me is unlike anything I have experienced. It heats my whole body, as if the blood underneath my skin is boiling, and my body convulses.

"I didn't want to use that, you have to see. Magic is not the way, not like this," Jordell says, voice trembling. He climbs onto his horse with difficulty; the magic seems to have drained him. "I'm sorry Jareb, truly I am. But I fear what that sorceress is feeding you, and I fear what you will become." Kicking his heels into the side of his steed, he sets off at pace before my guards can get to him.

Two guards help me to my feet. I can still feel my body twitching sporadically, and I feel a rage building up inside me. "Get off me." I push the guards away from me, not wanting to show any signs of weakness. "Don't just stand there, get after him! That man is a mage, and a traitor to the crown!"

Looking shaken at the news of a spell-caster within the city, five of my men rush to their horses and canter after Jordell. I swear by the gods he will hang for his treachery – for embarrassing me by escaping. Better yet, I may let Morgana have her way with him.

I dust myself down and limp back inside to rest. His magic has sapped my energy and my muscles ache tremendously. Looking up at the sky, I vow to myself that I will wield magic, that I will end this war.

I just need Jordell and that blasted spell book.

30
VĪREO

"I yield." The boy pants heavily from where he lies on ground. I have to hand it to him; he put up a sprightly fight.

"What's your name, boy?" Lek growls from behind me. "A fool to think you could challenge an adult when you are still just a pup."

"I like him. He can hide in the shadows, like me." Gillam says, chortling as she weighs up the scrawny lad sprawled out on the ground.

"I believe Lek has asked you a question." I keep my sword pointed at him just in case he has any other tricks up his sleeve.

"Laith. My name is Laith." His accent is surprisingly well-spoken, given his shambolic appearance.

"You look feral, boy. How is it you came to be here?" My sword is unwavering.

"You are one to talk, the state of you!" he spits back at me.

Lek and Gillam roar with laughter, something I do not appreciate. I contemplate driving my sword into the boy for his cheek, but instead I flick it to the side and cut Laith's clothing, to remind him how easily I could end him

"Be mindful of your tongue, boy."

"Oh, I like him," Gillam laughs. "I think we should keep him. Be mindful not to spike the boy, Vireo. He shows spirit."

I offer my hand and help him back to his feet. "Try to steal from us again and it will not end with laughter," I warn.

"I was hidden within the caravan that you ambushed," Laith says, finally answering my question.

"If you were there, then you would know that they attacked us first," I correct him.

"That is a matter of perspective." The confidence he exudes is something I would expect from someone much older than him.

I eye his malnourished frame, then retrieve some bread and water from the cart, which I pass to him. "You look like you need a good meal. Why were you with the caravan?"

"I am a squire. *Was* a squire," he corrects himself, his face falling. Something flashes across his face that I can't quite read, and I wonder if he is going to force another round of combat upon me. Instead, he takes a large bite out of the hardening bread and chews it wildly, then takes a large gulp of water. It must have been days since the boy last ate, and for a moment, I feel for him; until last night, I was hungry, too. Now I nurse a sore head from the fine wine we drank, and a swollen belly, feeling sympathy for a stranger.

The more I look at the boy as he makes his way through the stale bread and water, the more I feel I know him from somewhere. It irks me. I swear on my father's grave that we have crossed paths before, but I can't quite put my finger on it. I hop onto the back of the cart and let my legs swing over the edge, my sword placed by my side just in case the boy suddenly rushes me.

"You know who we are, don't you?" I press him, looking for answers.

"I've already told you, Jareb has posters with your faces on it all over Askela and the smaller villages." He cannot hide his contempt for me, which seems like a strange reaction to have toward someone just because of a bounty. No, I have wronged this boy in some way, and as long as I do not know how, he cannot be trusted.

"Tell me, boy, have we crossed paths before this day?" I reach for an apple within our supplies and take a large bite out of it.

"It takes an arrogant man to not know the faces of those that he has wronged. Do you have such disregard for others?" the boy says, not bothering to hide his hatred. "It was not so long ago that I met you. Your attention was not on me, though."

It snaps into my head, like a branch breaking. "The knight. You said you were a squire. Were you Orjan's?" My mind goes back to the day outside the Great Temple, where I collected a long-standing debt from the man.

The boy's eyes well, which surprises me. He lowers his bread, his body tensing.

"If you are his squire, why are you here? It is a knight's duty to ensure that his squire is well-cared-for." It at least explains why the boy is so good with his weapon. Orjan is a skilled weapons master.

"I *was* his squire," the boy spits, and some chewed bread fires out of his mouth, such is the venom in his words.

"Was?" Gillam asks.

"That day outside the Great Temple, when you humiliated Orjan. He gave you all the coin he had, and you still beat him!" The boy's anger towards me continues to grow.

"I had to teach Orjan a lesson, one that I hope he remembers. It is not my fault your former master has an addiction to gambling with coin he does not have."

"Yet you were still wise enough to accept the bet even though you knew his circumstance." The boy has a fair point. I took the bet knowing Orjan's reputation, but I also knew that he would come through.

It's ironic, really; all that coin now sits in our camp, unusable. I am unable to spend it on any of the luxuries that I had planned for my new life with Allana.

"Because of you, he left that very day, saying I would be better off without him. I have been scavenging for scraps since."

"He's handy with a sword," Lek throws in. "Might be worth keeping him around."

"I agree with the oaf." Gillam walks towards the boy and plants her hand on his shoulder.

"What the blazes!" Lek shrieks. He drops to the floor, clutching his leg.

It is at this point I see an orange and black creature scurrying away through the fallen leaves. It has sharp needles on its back. Lek must have aggravated the creature somehow.

Instinctively, I crouch down and remove my blade, cutting the bottom part of Lek's pants to look at the wound. It is as I have thought – the needles on the back of the creature pierced his skin. Lek continues to howl in discomfort. The area is dark red, with purple blemishes forming around it at an alarming speed.

"That's a verum sting. Nasty little buggers," says Laith, inspecting the wound.

"A verum? How do you know this, boy?" Gillam asks, her voice laced with concern.

"Orjan taught me. That sting is going to turn nasty if you don't get the right potion for your friend. He could lose his leg."

Lek's face reddens from the pain. I have known this man since I was a child and never once heard him squeal in pain like he is now. My mind races. How can we find the correct potion to heal Lek's injured leg in time?

"If we step foot in Askela, we will be killed on sight," Gillam points out.

I look at the boy. He is our only option right now. "Laith, I have a favour to ask."

"Really? Why should I do anything for you?" His cockiness irks me, but we have no other options right now.

"Because I will pay you for your troubles and give you enough supplies to be on your way."

"And a horse?"

I need this potion if Lek is to keep his leg. "Yes, and a horse."

"Are you mad, Vireo? What's to say this boy won't just leave with his coin and horse in tow?" Gillam appears less than impressed with my request, but I see no other way. We must trust the boy.

"Because he is the squire of a knight and thus duty-bound to carry out this request, or risk losing any honour he has," I spit. The bylaws of knights are convoluted and lengthy, but I spent some time studying their ways when I was younger.

I throw the boy a small bag of coin, which should be more than enough to get the potion we require. "I'll double it when you get back with the potion."

Laith throws me a smile as he places the coin inside his worn tunic and grabs one of the steeds.

"Head to the Great Temple," I call to him as he climbs on Lek's horse. "Ask for Jordell, he is a healer."

I watch him ride away. Now all we can do is wait.

And hope he returns.

31

VIREO

I pace back and forth.

Lek sits to my right, propped up by a large tree. His eyes are closed and flickering, his mutterings becoming words of insanity as his body fights desperately against the poison that courses through his veins.

The boy has been gone for nearly five hours, and I worry for Lek's fate. The skin on his lower leg blisters and weeps, and the discolouration seems to be spreading. The immediate area where the needle stuck is crusted, and on the outer edge a black line forms. I have been on the battlefield enough times to understand that his skin is dying. If the boy does not hurry, Lek will not only lose his leg, but also his life.

"Vireo?" Lek stutters, opening his eyes. His voice rasps as if liquid lines his windpipes.

"I am here, old boy," I reassure him. "How are you feeling?"

"My leg is on fire and my body aches. Never been better." He forces a smile, trying to lift my mood, but I cannot hide the concern on my face.

Lek is my brother, and I need him to pull through this, to be ok. We have been through far too much for his life to be taken in this way, and I will not have it. I will not let him be taken by this place.

"You will survive this, brother. We will survive this."

"The boy has fled with our coin, Vireo," Gillam calls from the shadows, "and you allowed it." She stands guard on the edge of camp against the hidden dangers of the dark forest.

"Now is not the time, Gillam," I snap – but her words reflect my own worries: what if the boy isn't coming back?

Lek musters a laugh. "You would have me thinking you are more bothered about the gold and my horse than my health." His laugh quickly evolves into coughing. "Who would have thought that I would be bested by something so small."

A wry smile forms on Gillam's lips. "That's because I *am* more bothered about the coin."

Lek grimaces. "I can't carry on like this, Vireo." He struggles to form the words, as if the pain is too much for him to bear.

I squeeze his hand, my jaw clenched. "Brother, you are going to be ok," I tell him, but I feel like my words are more for my comfort than his.

"Admit it, Vireo, the boy is not coming back," Gillam says. I know she blames me for the situation we find ourselves in, and she is not wrong. "Vireo, we must remove his leg."

"No, the boy will come good."

Lek coughs and his breathing becomes more laboured as he gasps for air. He grabs the scruff of my tunic, pulling me closer to him. I am surprised at his strength given his current state, but I listen intently to what he wishes to tell me.

"Take it. Take the leg."

"No, Lek! We must hold out for the boy."

"By then, the poison might be too far gone. I would rather lose my leg than my life."

Lek pushes me away from him. I move towards the fire that sits in the centre of our camp and pick up my sword.

This is all my fault. First Allana, and now Lek. Is this my fate – to be tormented by their deaths?

"Gillam, light a torch."

Gillam does as I ask. Around us, I hear nothing. No rustling trees, no creatures from within the forest. Everything is silent as I approach Lek, clutching my sword.

He watches me and says nothing, as if he has accepted his fate.

I rip some of the tunic from my arm and roll the fabric up, then pass it to Lek. "Bite down on this."

There is still a spark in his eye, but it is clear he just wants the pain to end. When I lift the blade above my head, the steel almost feels weightless. Numbness takes over as I focus on what I must do.

I can hear muffled words from behind me, but I can't quite make them out. Then the words get louder and louder until it pierces my tranced state.

"Over there, Vireo!" Gillam is shouting at me.

I snap back to myself. There is movement in the trees, the pounding of a galloping horse.

It feels like an eternity, but I recognise the shape of Lek's large horse.

Laith has returned. But there is another figure on the horse with him.

Jordell.

32
VIREO

Wielding magic leaves you feeling euphoric, as if no feat is too hard. It is afterwards when that feeling fades that you begin to truly understand the consequence of your actions.
-Harriet Clem, KR 220

Laith has a busted lip and Jordell has a wound to the top of his head, with dried blood matted into his hair and down the left side of his face. His eye is swollen, and his already dishevelled clothing is muddied and torn. He carries a large satchel.

"Thank the gods you are here." I breathe a huge sigh of relief and lower my sword. "I presume you ran into trouble, looking at the state of you both."

"It would appear that the healer has made an enemy of the crown," Laith explains as he brings his horse to a stop.

Jordell climbs down and immediately moves towards Lek. "If it was not for Laith, I fear I would be confined to the depths of Jareb's dungeons, or worse, to that vile sorceress's experiments. I will explain shortly, but time is of the essence." Jordell places his satchel on the ground next to Lek and pulls out some small vials. He uses a mortar and pestle to grind some herbs into a paste with impressive speed. "This will help with the pain." Jordell wraps the paste in a leaf to form a small parcel and places this into Lek's mouth. "Chew it a few times, then swallow. You will feel its effects sooner. I can only apologise for the taste, but needs must."

Lek does as he is told and chews, his expression one of disgust as he forces it down. Jordell inspects his leg and shakes his head.

"I am sorry, but the poison runs too deep. There is no potion that I can concoct that will save his leg."

Looking down at the sword in my hand, I know I must hasten if we are to save Lek's life.

"What are you doing?" Jordell presses.

"What I must."

"I said there isn't a potion I can concoct to save his leg. I didn't say I couldn't save his leg." Jordell reaches into his bag and pulls out the spell book we had given him to transcribe.

He flicks through the pages, his eyes scanning over the text like a madman, one who knows what he is looking for.

"You can't have transcribed that text already," I say, amazed.

Jordell runs his hand frantically over the pages until he stops and presses his finger against a section of text. I pray to the gods that whatever he plans is going to work; it has to.

Jordell places his hand over Lek's leg and begins an incantation. *"Thorto, spregu, sintum, fedus."* Jordell's hand glows. *"Thorto, spregu, sintum, fedus."*

Lek recoils in pain and attempts to pull his leg away, almost knocking the healer over, but Jordell keeps his balance and his hand in place.

"Over here, boy, you need to help me!" I say, waving Laith over. Together, we restrain the giant man, which is like fighting a wild bear. Whatever pain Lek was in prior to the healer casting his spell, it must pale in comparison to what he feels now, judging by his screams.

Both Jordell and Lek shake violently, and Jordell looks as though it is taking every ounce of effort to maintain contact with the wound.

"*Thorto, spregu, sintum, fedus!*" He calls out again.

I feel my eyes widen at what I am witnessing. The red infection draws back down Lek's leg, the disgusting blisters shrinking. The poison visibly moves towards Jordell's hand. It looks as though he is drawing it all back to one point. Raising his hand, I can see the poison is now pooled in one bulbous area.

"*Intumgara!*" Jordell yells as the poison comes away from Lek's body and hangs in the air. Jordell then moves towards the fire, bringing the poison with him. All the while, dark liquid is moving closer to Jordell's hand. He needs to move faster. The healer launches his hand towards the fire and the poison is hurled across like a wet stone. The flames lash the air wildly as they consume the poison, and Jordell drops to his knees.

Looking down at Lek, I see he has passed out from the pain, but his leg has – miraculously – returned to normal.

"Thank you," I say to a weary-looking Jordell. Then I nod towards the boy. "My thanks are to be shared with you, too. It seems you are a man of your word."

"So it would seem." The boy smirks as he helps Jordell to his feet. "Are you ok?" He asks sincerely.

"I assume so," Jordell says. "This is all new to me. Until I fully understand that book, I will not know the consequences of the forces I now find myself dabbling in." He pants heavily, as though he has been running for a prolonged period. Sweat beads on his head and his face looks reddened and worn.

I grab a bottle of wine from the back of the cart and pull the cork out with my teeth, spitting it on the ground. Then I pass the bottle to Jordell. "Here, drink some of this. I am no mage, but I can tell you that drinking this will make you feel better."

Jordell smiles, accepting the bottle. He takes a large gulp, then breathes an exaggerated sigh of relief.

"Thank you," I tell him again. "I – we – are indebted to you for your help."

"You do not need to thank me, Vireo. I do what I can because I have the ability to help others. I fear that not doing so could send me on a darkened path." Jordell takes another large gulp of wine before passing the bottle back to me. His hand is shaking wildly. He needs to rest.

I take a drink of the wine to steady my own nerves before passing it to Laith.

"You did well, boy," says Gillam from the far side of the camp, her focus still on the trees. "I will not lie; I did not think you would return." Now she looks at me. "Now, however, we have almost double the number of mouths to feed."

I understand her concern, but I do not respond. Instead, I gesture at Jordell's bloodied head and bruised eye. "May I ask what led to your current state? I mean, prior to helping Lek." He looks in a right state, his body battered and worn.

Jordell stares into the fire, warming his tremoring hands by the flames. His eyes look vacant, as if he is looking into something beyond its sparks. "Jareb. He finds himself in a bleak place since Lady Allana's death. He has turned to dark magic under the influence of a vile sorceress." He pauses, as if gathering his thoughts. "I walked to the dungeons, having transcribed some of the pages, and it is a horrible place at the best of times. But what I saw" – he trips on his words – "what I saw down there was nothing short of evil. Jareb is imprisoning people for non-payment of taxes. Once there, he is letting his sorceress carry out all manner of experiments on them. I had the displeasure of walking in on one of them. She killed a man by transferring another's wound onto him. When I agreed to transcribe this book, I did it because I wanted to help others. If I had told them what I had discovered in the book, I dread to think what she could do with her magic. With her witchcraft."

This is a lot to take in, and my thoughts recoil in horror at what Jareb is doing. I cannot help but feel that this is my doing. After all, it is I who pushed Jareb past breaking point, past the point of no return.

"There's a reason why magic is outlawed and that those who wield it are imprisoned," Jordell continues. "The slightest use can create crippling addiction. As you can see in myself, using it takes its toll on the body. The after-effect is unknown until the spell is cast." Jordell rubs his hands together over the fire. Laith passes Jordell the wine again, and he drinks.

"In the dungeon, they were working on a way to pass that infliction onto others, by way of using other people's lives as a conduit. Jareb believes that this is how they will end the king's war, but it is not. I see his sorceress becoming more powerful until eventually no one can stop her. She is dangerous, Vireo, and when I saw what they were doing, I knew I had to leave. I escaped the grounds of the castle and got to the Great Temple where I intended to gather some items. Jareb's men were quickly upon me. I fear where I would be now, had Laith not arrived when he did. The two of us were able to fight our way out of the temple and he brought me here, explaining what had happened to one of your men."

"We are not his to command," Gillam spits from the shadows.

I offer my hand to Jordell. "You need to rest. Use my things in the cart. It will provide shelter, warmth, and comfort until you are stronger." I pull him to his feet.

"Thank you," he says.

I can't help but notice the limp he now carries, one which I didn't notice him having before.

33

JAREB

My dreams take me to darkened places where I relive the night that Allana's life ended. My body is sleep deprived and malnourished. It is affecting my mind and the decisions that I make, further worsened by the voice that keeps piercing my thoughts. As I dry myself in my bath chambers, I see that my physique is diminished with the weight loss I have endured over the past few weeks. When I pull on my tunic, I feel the fabric hang loose over my body.

I stare at the other side of the bath chamber where Allana would normally ready herself in the morning, with her perfect body submerged in the water where I had often joined her. Then anger surges through me as I wonder whether Allana shared these chambers with *him*.

This happens every day, now – memories of my perfectly beautiful wife surfacing, only to be tainted by the thoughts of that vermin tarnishing her. Defiling her. All while they laughed at me and concocted their plan to escape to a new life.

Now I find myself here again. Alone, angry, and

betrayed. I know that the thoughts behind my decline are twisted, but I cannot fight them. The need I once had to satisfy others is gone, and in its place, only a blackened heart remains. One which will do whatever it takes to end this war, so that I need not have to govern the people of Askela any longer. So that I can remove myself to a life of solitude.

I want to be left alone, but this kingdom will not rule itself.

Taxes have been paid on time and in full since I took a stronger approach towards those that failed to pay. It amazes me how people can provide the coin after all, when the right motivation is applied.

It surprises me most mages have been thus far reluctant to come forward, but a handful of mages have lent themselves to the cause, accepting my offer of further training and reward. They will be given land and sufficient coin to live well once the war is over.

We still don't have that spell book, though. Jordell's actions have led to the prolonged torture of the criminals holed up in the dungeon. If only he knew people were suffering because of his selfishness.

Outside, I pass through the wintry courtyard, my cold breath rising in the air. I must send word to the king with an update on my progress, but I am not keen on divulging too much information. My cousin is a proud man and would recoil at the thought of magic being cultivated within his castle walls by way of torture. Still, I will tell him of my intentions, but not until we are strong enough and I can convince him we will tip the balance of war in our favour.

A scribe waits for me at a table in the summons room, parchment and quill laid out in front of him. He is middle-aged with greying hair tied back, his white tunic carrying the golden symbol of the king.

"Sire," the scribe greets me by standing and nodding as I enter the room.

"Shall we get started?" I begin walking the length of the room as I dictate to the scribe. "Dear Cousin, the people of Askela have pulled together and provided the coin that is needed to aid the war. We have sent the coin along with food and weapons to continue to aid you in this holy war."

The scribe dips his quill into the ink and etches my spoken words onto the parchment.

"The people fare well, and we are all glad to contribute what we can. If there is anything else that you need, please let me know. I am happy to oblige any further requests." My words repulse me. I am sickened at the feigned gratitude I must show in order to feed my brute of a cousin's ego. What I want to tell him and what I can tell him are two different things. I would be dead before long if I truly spoke my mind.

The scribe continues to write my words as I dictate a few more niceties rather than the bile I force myself not to spew. When the scribe is finished, I take the quill and sign the bottom of the letter. The scribe blows on the ink for a moment, then places it in an envelope and pours wax over the overlap, pressing it down with the family crest.

"Get that to the messenger right away," I say. The scribe bows his head and leaves, and I sit down at the desk to gather my thoughts.

There is a firm, brisk knock at the door. It startles me.

"Come in," I sigh at my moment of silence being disturbed.

Codrin enters, his frame filling the doorway. "Sire, I have news."

"Go on?"

"Lord Vek's caravan was ambushed on the way to Entaria. The reports say three men caught them unaware, ambushing them from inside the Forest of Opiya."

"Vireo," I growl. "When did this happen?" And how on earth have they survived this long?

"Six days ago, sire. Lord Vek sent word as soon as he arrived in Entaria. By all accounts he is furious. What would you have me do?" Codrin stands well over six feet tall and towers over me. The man looks like a mountain compared to me, and I find that being overshadowed in such a way makes me feel uneasy.

"None of our men will step foot in that place. It is a death wish. No one can survive in that wretched place for long." I cannot afford to waste my guards. I do not have the manpower to hunt him down. "For the time being, we will have to wait. Alert the guards and circulate the bounty for Vireo and his men around Levanthria. I want the reward known to every city and town. Five hundred crowns for his head. Two hundred for those who aid him."

"There's more, sire. Our scout's report that Jordell was last seen heading to the Forest of Opiya himself. It seems he may have set up camp there with Vireo." Codrin's face is stern and unmoving, showing no emotion as he gives his report.

"So it seems." I wave Codrin away as I muse over my thoughts. Had they been planning this all along, or is this simply the hand that fate has given us?

"*It is meant to be this way,*" a familiar voice only I can hear hisses in my mind.

34
VIREO

It takes a powerful person to master magic. It takes an even stronger person to wean yourself from its grasp. To stop the power coursing through your veins even when your body craves it; that is true strength.

-Zaphire Etsom, alchemist, Temple Of Eltera 254 KR

Laith, Gillam, and I are perched on logs around the fire while Jordell prepares ingredients for stew, and the warmth of the flames press against my legs. It is proving beneficial to have Jordell around camp – as it turns out, Jordell is as skilled a cook as he is an alchemist. It may not be to the standards we are accustomed to, but there can be no denying that since he took over preparing our food, it has improved in taste.

Laith, too, seems keen to prove himself, more so to Gillam than me. When he isn't doing supply runs, he trains with her, even adapting his sword stance to incorporate Gillam's style and speed. All he asks for in exchange is that any leftover coin be shared with the people of Askela.

Lek, Gillam, and I take turns with watch duty so that Jordell can focus on transcribing the spell book. Other than the odd small creature passing through, we remain undisturbed by the larger beasts that we believe roam this enchanted forest.

"Is that really how you three met?" Laith asks, smiling with delight. Gillam has just finished regaling him with stories of our past.

"I swear it is true." Gillam raises the bottle in her hand and takes a swig of the sweet wine before passing it across the fire to Laith. "Have I told you about the time we caught Lek in a compromising position with a pig?"

"If you value your life, Gillam, I suggest you end this story here," Lek calls from the edge of camp where he has taken up watch.

Laith fights to stop himself from spitting his wine into the fire. "Now you must me."

Gillam lowers her voice. "Let's just say that Lek went into a barn with a woman he had met in a town just north of Eltera. The ale flowed, and both were more than merry as they went about to have at it. Unfortunately for Lek, his company had passed out, and being in such a drunken stupor, it was not her that his hands were wandering over."

"Not that there was much difference between the pig and his company," I add.

The three off us try and suppress our laughs into a snigger so that Lek does not hear us.

"I dread to think where that would have ended up had we not intervened," says Gillam. She takes the bottle from Laith and finishes it off before casting it into the trees.

"I have so many more stories about that oaf," she continues, beaming. The flames of the fire catch her eyes in the moment. It is rare for Gillam to let her hair down in this manner. Normally her style is to get blind drunk, find a man or woman to have her way with, and then leave. To see her laughing and telling tales of old is quite refreshing to see, and I smile. "Even more about this one." She turns the attention onto me.

"And I would say that's enough stories for one evening," I chuckle, stopping her in her tracks – no need to diminish Laith's opinion of me just yet. The woman knows far too much about me and the compromising positions I have been found in over the years.

Suddenly, something flies through the air and smashes into the side of Gillam's head. It is the wine bottle she tossed into the trees only moments before.

I leap to my feet. Blood oozes from a cut to the left of her hairline and begins to drip down her face. Her smile is immediately replaced with contorted anger.

"What the fuck was that for, Lek?"

I open my mouth to tell her I'm fairly certain Lek isn't the perpetrator, but before I can get the words out, something large stomps into camp.

"OGRE!" Lek bellows. Its frame stands a good foot or two taller than even Lek. Its large, thickened head has two protruding teeth from the bottom of its mouth. It only has one eye; a sunken hole has replaced the other, and a clawed scar shows how the beast came to lose it. The ogre is bare-chested, revealing protruding bones from its body. Its skin has somehow healed around the bones, forming ivory spikes. In its hand it clutches a log, which it swings as Lek approaches.

Lek ducks and brandishes his great axe, making to bring a swift end to the creature. Ogres are not easy to slay – their skin is renowned for its thickness – but I can't see how a blow from Lek's axe wouldn't be able to penetrate its skin.

He doesn't have the chance to land a blow, however, because the ogre grabs his axe with his free hand, jarring Lek to a halt. Lek tries to wrestle the axe from the monster, but the ogre's strength far surpasses his own. The ogre draws Lek into the air, bringing his face level with its one eye. With an almighty battle roar, it hurtles him towards us as if he weighs nothing. Embers spray us as Lek rolls through the fire before sliding to a halt, groaning in pain. Laith, Gillam, and I stand dumbfounded at what we have just seen.

Jordell lets the vegetables scatter to the ground as he hurries to our side, a kitchen knife in his hand. My mind races as I try to think of the best way to fell this creature. A kitchen knife certainly isn't going to do it.

"What do we do now?" Laith grips his blade in both hands, his voice trembling with adrenaline. I am impressed that in the face of such danger, he doesn't consider running.

"We pray to the gods," Jordell answers.

"Is there any magic you can use?" Gillam asks.

"As much as I want to, I can't. If I overuse it, the burden on my body will be too much."

The ogre growls, casting its eyes on us.

"Well, we won't be around much longer if you don't!" Gillam shouts.

I squeeze the hilt of my blade. Within seconds, the ogre is on us. It brings its snarling rage down us with a blow from the tree trunk in its hand. I dive to the side, barely dodging the bludgeon. The ground rumbles as the enormous weapon hits the ground, spraying earth everywhere.

I glance towards the others. Jordell is sprawled out in the dirt and Laith looks determined but unscathed. As Gillam attempts to stand, the ogre cuffs her with the back of its hand, which sends her my way. I break her fall, but we both land in a crumpled heap as Gillam gasps for air, her face a bloodied mess from the gash on her head.

"Sprightly, isn't it?" She scoops up her dagger and runs straight for the ogre, and before the beast can react, she rams her blade into its leg. A low rumble escapes the ogre before it slaps Gillam down to the ground again. She has done her bit, though, and her dagger protrudes from the beast's leg, blood flowing from the new wound.

The ogre uses its free hand to remove the blade and then pitches it at me. It soars towards me at a frightening pace, but bounces in front of me as if it has hit a wall. Jordell has somehow deflected it with a spell, removing the weapon's momentum.

"I thought you couldn't cast," I say, though I'm grateful; the mage just saved my life.

"A deflection spell doesn't use up too much energy. I should be ok."

The ogre attempts to step on Gillam, who is struggling on the ground beside it. Lek shoots his hand out and grabs her by the ankle, dragging Gillam helplessly through the dirt.

"What do we do?" Laith shouts. He maintains his offensive stance, ready to strike.

There is crashing in the trees behind the ogre and I dread what else is about to greet us.

I don't see any other choice. "Run!" I command the others. There's no way we can take on a second one.

But it isn't another ogre.

Growls fill the air as a pack of wolfaires surround us. Their matted fur stands on edge and they emit an aggressive rumble, preparing for a fight. I count at least eight as they begin to circle the ogre, led by the familiar black alpha.

He produces a prolonged growl which transforms into a snarl as he bares its teeth at the ogre, snapping at its legs. The ogre weighs up the situation, and growls back itself before turning and heading into the trees.

The alpha turns to face me and bows his head. I stare into his eyes, frozen in place by a mixture of fear and wonder. Then he raises his head to the moon above and releases an eery howl. The other wolfaires follow suit and bay into the night sky.

Then they dart back into the woods.

This is the second time the wolfaire has protected us. My only question now is – why?

35
VIREO

The day after the encounter with the ogre, Laith leaves on a supply run, and we hang back in camp, a quiet anxiety having taken hold. The attack was a reminder of how dangerous the forest really is. Soon, we may have to make a decision: continue to live at the mercy of the monsters within the forest – or put ourselves at the mercy of the monsters in the city.

I can't decide which sounds worse.

Jordell is finishing off some food for us all. The rich smell worsens my hunger pains as the stew bubbles in a pot over the fire. He seems to have recovered from the wounds he sustained during his escape from Askela, but the limp remains.

The alchemist ladles some of the stew into Lek's outstretched bowl, and Lek carries it with him to the edge of camp where he takes up position for his watch.

"Here you go." Jordell passes me a dish. It smells divine – and if it smells good, it tastes even better. My senses go into overload as I take in the broth. I am not sure if it's Jordell's cooking or my hunger, but the stew rivals anything Choa would have made for me at home. I wonder whatever happened to my cook. Or my estate, for that matter.

Gillam sits quietly. Her hair sticks to her cheek from congealed blood. She hasn't said a word to me since the ogre attack, but at least she engages with the others.

She cannot stay mad at me forever.

Jordell passes Gillam some stew and eyes her appearance. "We really need to get that sorted," he says, his face full of concern.

"Is there not a spell you can use and be done with it?" She asks.

"I am afraid I must conserve my energy for when the time calls. For now, it is nothing that a needle and some thread can't fix." Jordell examines the deep cut through Gillam's blood-encrusted hair. "Let me clean it, before it becomes infected," he says.

"I'll be fine with some food and some wine," Gillam mutters, bringing the bowl to her mouth and slurping loudly. She winces in the process. "Good thing those wolfaires showed up when they did."

Jordell sighs, but says nothing more of her wound. "I have never seen or heard of anything like that before," he says instead, seating himself on Lek's vacated log. "Wild wolfaires protecting men against a monster of the forest? The gods must be playing games with us."

"It is not the first time we have crossed paths with them," I explain. "In fact, the last time we saw the alpha, he stopped the pack from tearing us from limb to limb."

"How strange, that such a creature would show such protective instincts to the group." Jordell sips his stew and closes his eyes.

"It's no coincidence," says Gillam. "That alpha has

turned up and protected us ever since that day you rescued it from that snare."

"What did you say?" Jordell asks a bit sharply. I frown, wondering if there is really any truth to that.

"Vireo saved that alpha when we were out hunting, before all of this happened."

"That's very interesting." Jordell seems lost in thought for a moment. "It would appear that your act of kindness has borne fruit."

"So it would appear," I say, finishing my stew. It's not the first time I have wondered this myself. Has the wolfaire been keeping these creatures at bay all this time?

Then I hear the steady sound of horse hoofs hitting the forest floor. Within a moment, Laith returns, and he is a welcome sight; with our stores running low, we need all the supplies we can get. I smile in his direction, but then I see his face. He wears an expression of concern and sorrow.

"Is everything ok, Laith?" Jordell gets up and takes the reins, steadying the steed as the boy dismounts.

"I am afraid there's not much supplies from this run," he says. "Askela is not in a good state."

"What do you mean?" Jordell asks before I have time to pose the same question.

"I mean, that coward of a leader has led the city into an even worse state than it was already in." Laith removes the parcels that lay over the back of his horse. "The people of Askela are starving, Jordell. Jareb is bleeding them dry. No one has much to trade. Worse still, he is still sending those who cannot pay to the dungeons. What I have been able to fetch will only last us one or two days. I must head straight back out. Vireo, may I take some more coin?"

Previously, the woes of the poor would not have affected me. I avert my eyes, because we all know that the hardships people are facing is partly due to my own actions. Furthermore, we cannot survive for much longer like this.

"We need to make this camp more sustainable, if we are to survive," I say, thinking out loud.

Without warning, Laith rushes at me and pushes me backwards with a good amount of force. I barely manage to plant my feet and prevent myself from toppling over.

"I tell you what is going on in Askela, and this is how you respond? You care only for yourself," he spits. His fury catches me off guard.

Gillam jumps into the fray and wraps her hands around the boy. "Calm down," she scolds, "you will draw more creatures out to us."

"What's going on over there?" Lek calls.

"Just Vireo getting his arse handed to him by Laith," Gillam chortles.

"I understand your frustrations, boy," I tell him, and I mean it. "Think of it this way: if we are dead, then no one will help the people of Askela."

"And how do you propose we help them, Vireo?" Jordell asks me. He is clearly concerned for the people whom, under normal circumstances, he would be tending to.

"As I said before the boy lost his head, we need to make this camp more sustainable."

"We need seeds to sow our own food," Jordell says, catching on. "Make this a more permanent setting for us."

"The fewer times we travel into Askela, the better. There is a bounty on all our heads except Laith's," I remind the group.

"Maybe it's a bounty worth cashing in. I can then give that coin to people who need it more than us," Laith says, glaring at me with disgust.

Gillam strikes him, and the boy falls to the ground. "Gather yourself, Laith. You need to get a grip on that temper of yours. You will get us all killed at this rate. Or get yourself killed." I see Gillam's threat as genuine. It is not as though she has been waiting for an excuse to kill someone. Laith spits blood from his mouth.

Jordell furrows his brows. "The Great Temple will no doubt be ransacked by Jareb's men looking for anything that can be used in their mission to unlock magic. However, there is a chance that some of my effects may still be in my study."

"Like what?" I ask.

"Like the seeds of plants and vegetables that we will need if we are, in fact, to make this place more sustainable. I have a great collection which I store in part of the library, sealed away. I can't see them taking seeds, as they would prove relatively useless unless concocting healing potions. What's more, I am in dire need of some items to clean up that nasty gash on Gillam's head. It will soon be infected if it is not properly cleaned and sealed," Jordell finishes.

"Then we have a plan. We just need to think about how we get into the city," I say.

"I will go!" The boy proclaims.

I hesitate. He is angry, and I wouldn't put it past him to cash in on that coin. It would be rash to send him in this state. Besides, he looks exhausted from his travels and seems in good need of rest. Perhaps then he will be more reasonable.

"Gillam and I will go. Gillam is the master of the shadows, so she'll be able to easily find us a way in undetected. With the two of us together, there is less chance of us being captured."

Gillam pulls up the red hood that hangs from her cloak.

"I agree with Vireo. We should be able to get in and out relatively easy. Providing we are not detected by the guards."

"Easier said than done, but as the day grows darker, this is a good window of opportunity for us," Jordell says. "What are we going to do about the people of Askela though, Vireo? We cannot leave them in such hardship."

I have an idea for this, one that will keep Lek and Gillam happy as well as Jordell and Laith. I pick up a large bag of coin from the back of the cart, far more than we have been sending the boy to trade with. I carry it across to my horse and place it into the satchel that sits on the back of the saddle.

"What on earth are you doing with our coin?" Lek calls, hearing the coins jingling in their bag.

"Consider it an investment," I say. "If we provide coin for people who need it, they are more likely to help us and not hand us over to the guards." Although the coin I carry is less than the reward being offered for our heads, I hope and pray that perceived kindness will win them over. "Who knows what a little kindness can reap for us." I picture the wolfaire, who has preserved our lives simply because of one kind gesture.

"Although I don't agree with your morals, Vireo, I am agreeable to the sharing of that coin for people in need. If this is what you must do, you have my blessing." Jordell waves his hand over us while muttering some religious jargon.

I reach into the other side of my satchel and remove Allana's emerald hood, the heavily torn cloak draping down beneath it. I pull it over my head and breathe in her scent that is still embedded within it. It brings me comfort, but it will also help me shield my face in the darkness. If there is one thing I have learnt in the last day from the wolfaire, it is that a little kindness can go a long way. If I can do the same for the people of Askela, maybe we will be able to find a way home.

Mounting our horses, Gillam and I head into the trees, to Askela.

36

JAREB

It is a crisp, chilly night. Large clouds linger in the air, blocking out the moon, providing a darkened blanket over Askela. I find myself restless in my bed. Not even the company of two chambermaids has granted me enough comfort to sleep for a full night. The ringing in my ears is constant and painful, a high-pitched noise that seems to worsen with every day that passes.

I don't know the names of the two women who lie sprawled across my bed as if they offer some form of decoration. Both women are beautiful. The one on the left has short blonde hair that reveals her pointed elven ears, her skin as pale as ice. The woman she is spooning has long, dark hair and a slim face. I found myself drawn to her fire-like amber eyes the evening prior. We had a pleasant night, I enjoyed the wine and the company. But, still unable to sleep, I now stand on the balcony, looking over Askela.

Planting my hands on the freezing stone edge, I lean forward and look down. It must be around a one-hundred-foot drop to the bottom. As I stare into the abyss below me, I contemplate climbing onto the railing. It would be a sure plummet to my death, but at least my mind would be at rest. The headaches would stop, as would this incessant ringing. I snap myself into the room and banish the dark thoughts, instead choosing to look up at the darkened sky and the shapes of the clouds.

I release an enormous sigh. What I wouldn't give for a full night's sleep, without seeing Allana's face or her death. Despite her treachery, I still find myself unable to move on, unable to banish her cruel face from my mind. The women that lie entangled in my bedsheets are proof of this. The two of them together have features that Allana possessed, but in truth, they pale in compared to my one true love.

"Are you ok, my lord?" I recognise the voice behind me straight away. Turning around, I see Morgana standing at the edge of my bed, her bright red hair tied up above her head. She wears a silver, translucent gown, leaving little to my imagination, the neck of which plunges far enough down to reveal the top of her stomach. I can see everything underneath, and I feel certain that this is her intention.

"I find myself unable to sleep," I tell her, trying not to be distracted by the parts of her body she has left on show. "I have tried remedies, wine, the pleasure of good company. None of it is working. I cannot sleep. I cannot close my eyes without seeing her."

"Betrayal can leave your mind in a fragile state. In death, you were seeking closure, but it torments you. It will continue to torment you until you eventually throw yourself off that balcony."

"Have you seen this? Is this a vision of yours?" I move away from the balcony, not wishing to tempt fate. I have no intention of ending my life this way.

Morgana floats across the room, her gown flowing through the air as if moved by wind, but there is no breeze.

"It is why I am here, my lord, to serve you, to help you in any way I can." She stands behind me now and whispers her words into my ears. The closer she moves, the more the ringing in my ears fades.

"What do you have in mind?" I know full well where this is heading, but my heart is beating in a way it hasn't for some time.

"I can help you sleep." Morgana lingers on the word *sleep*, snake-like in the way she speaks to me. "You can't move on past Allana. It is too soon for you. This is normal. It will take time."

Morgana circles me like I am the prey and she, the wild animal about to attack its dinner.

"Have you heard of glamour?" She whispers delicately.

"No."

Morgana stops in front of me and lets down her hair. She raises both hands, her fingertips touching to just below her chin. She then moves her hands over her face, over the top of her head, flowing through her hair.

My eyes widen as I watch her face change form, her hair darken. Her body morphs as she massages her hands slowly downwards, and I let out a gasp.

"A – a – Allana?" I feel confused. My dead wife stands before me. My chest pounds, my head whirls.

"Yes, my love?" She whispers back to me. Even her voice is the same.

"What witchcraft is this?" I ask, transfixed on Allana's – no, Morgana's – face.

"It is a glamour spell, my love. I am here to serve, here to help you. Right now, I want to help you sleep and prevent you from taking the path I have seen. It is why I am here." Morgana takes my hand and leads me to the bed where the other two women lie undisturbed. She encourages me to lie down, then removes her gown slowly.

My heart races. Sleep is not on my mind, but I do feel that my thoughts are clearer than they have been for a while. Best of all, for the first time in as long as I can remember, the headache that has tormented me for too long fades.

37
VIREO

There is an island far north of Yugo's Tears, one shrouded in a fog not made from the clouds nor the mist by the sea but by the gods themselves. Deep within that island, there is a natural spring, the waters of which are said to reverse the effect of magic use.

-Diary of Gregor Yerald, explorer and monster hunter, 260 KR

I pull the reins on my horse, bringing it to a stop, and Gillam pulls up next to me on the black horse she claimed from the so-called nobleman.

My cold breath rises in front of me. Looking over the eastern point of Askela, all I can see is darkened shadows. The moon is hidden behind clouds, which is perfect for what we aim to achieve.

"We need to move on foot from here, if we are to remain undetected." Gillam is the first to dismount from her horse. She leads it towards a cluster of trees.

On the ride over, Gillam pointed out that the eastern

point of the city would be our best option for getting in undetected. Jordell's study sits inside the Great Temple, which is just outside the centre of Askela. Despite its location in the slums, we have to assume that Jareb will have more guards there, with the chance that Jordell returns with the spell book.

"If we make our way to the farms on the outskirts, we will be able to use the houses and huts as cover until we reach the city," says Gillam as she ties her horse to a tree and crouches to feel the dirt under our feet. "Not the driest. Could be worse though." Her face is hidden within the shadows of her red hood.

I follow suit and dismount my horse before wrapping the reins around the tree. The guards do not patrol this far out of the city, so our primary concern is that they be taken by others who just happen to be passing, or bandits.

I pull Allana's hood over the bottom half of my face, and the two of us set off towards Askela. Gliding through the fields quickly, we use the farmhouses as cover, to good effect. Within thirty minutes, we have reached the outer walls of the city. At the top of the wall, we hear the mumbled words of the guards that are standing watch through the night. The outer wall stands around forty feet tall, a distance from which the guards could easily see us if there were sufficient lighting. To our blessing, the clouds prevent the moon from lighting us up like a torch for all to see.

Standing with our backs against the wall, we slide sideways for ten minutes until we reach our intended target, the drainage gutters. Not the most elegant of entrances but an entranceway nonetheless. To my relief, the weather has not been stormy recently, so there is minimal water passing down through the gutter. I follow Gillam's lead towards the grid and turn sideways, squeezing my way through the rusted metal bars. The water passes just over my ankles, but the boots I wear shield my feet.

We are in the city. Now we just need to navigate the streets while remaining undetected.

I fall in step behind Gillam, who is really proving her worth as a master of the shadows.

Gillam lets out the occasional groan or tut as I travel more noisily than she would like. Meanwhile, she glides across the sodden ground, almost spirit-like. I fare well for longer periods but then find myself causing a splash in the odd puddle that is larger than I realised, much to Gillam's dismay.

There are around twenty guards on patrols in this area, each set up in twos or threes. It doesn't take Gillam long to figure out their route, which gives us the advantage. Unbeknownst to them, we hide in the shadows, slowly making progress. As a patrol passes nearby, Gillam gestures for me to get cover. I crouch behind the back of the house nearest to me, while she kneels in a ginnel just ahead.

The two guards stop suddenly. I wait with bated breath, wondering if they have heard something that drew their attention.

"Wait here for one minute, I need to take a piss," the larger of the two guards announces. To my dismay, he heads straight towards Gillam's hiding spot.

The guard steps into the alleyway and unloads his bladder, standing within touching distance from Gillam. I place my hand over the cold hilt of my sword and hold my breath, ready to attack. I can't help but think he must be bursting for the length of time he empties himself. The guard finishes up before rejoining his partner, and the two of them set off on their patrol once more.

To think that guard did not know how close he was to greeting death.

Once the guards have moved on, we continue until eventually we reach the outskirts of the city centre, to the road that takes us to the Great Temple.

Nothing prepares me for what I see when we arrive.

There are scores of people outside, sleeping rough. The houses on the outer edge are falling apart in a state of decay, and many have made ramshackle huts from scraps. It was bad before we fled Askela, but I am shocked by the number of shanty houses clustered together, dimly lit by small fires people have made to keep warm on this cold night.

Ahead of us stands the Great Temple, its doors and windows boarded up with planks of wood. Two guards stand at the entranceway. Even in these times of hardship, the people are prevented from using the empty halls of the temple to keep themselves warm and safe at night. I then recall the hall being full of sick men, women, and children, and I wonder what fate has been bestowed upon them with no one to tend to their ailments.

Gillam continues to lead, and we move around the back of the temple as quietly as possible. Jordell has instructed us to find a hidden trap door which should get us inside. We look for the shrubs that Jordell has briefed us on, which are easy enough to find. The door is there.

We prise the door open slowly, not wishing to draw any attention to ourselves, then drop inside.

All we need to do now is navigate this darkened passage, get what we came for, and get out of Askela.

It is safe to say that we have only just made it through the easiest part of our plan.

38
VIREO

Once inside, I lower Allana's hood to allow myself to breathe better. The air is damp and mouldy down here, but the scent of Allana's perfume masks this well. I can't see Gillam because of the darkness, but I know she is ahead of me in the tunnel. I feel my way down the hidden passage with both hands until I can see a slight gap between us where the smallest amount of light is forcing its way through – another trapdoor.

I bump into Gillam, who has stopped in her tracks.

"Do you smell that, Vireo?"

I press up against the panel above us, the trapdoor just big enough for us to squeeze through. Gillam offers her hands out to give me a boost up, and I pull myself up through the opening.

Nothing could have prepared me for the rancid aroma that greets me. I gag, then pull my hood back up over my face to mask it, but it still seeps through the fabric. The smell burns my nostrils, and I can't help but cough, my eyes watering wildly as I stop myself from vomiting.

"It smells of death up here," I whisper as I take hold of

Gillam's outstretched arm and pull her up. She cannot hide her repulsion at the smell, and draws her hood over the lower half of her face.

We are in a basement cluttered with wine racks and ale barrels. I grab one of the bottles of spirits and take a large gulp to steady my nerves, preparing myself for what may lie ahead. I pass the bottle to Gillam, and she toasts it in the air before taking an equally large gulp.

We continue through the cellar until we reach some large stone steps. With each step that we take, the smell grows stronger. When we reach the top, there is a buzzing noise on the other side of the door. I take a deep breath and push the door ajar with my shoulder, peeking inside.

The sight takes my breath away. We have seen all manner of death on the battlefield, but this is something else.

At least twenty bodies lie strewn across the makeshift tables that Jordell had fashioned into beds for the sick. More decomposing corpses are piled on the floor in a cloud of black flies. When we step through the door, we are engulfed by the swarm.

"What in the blazes is this hell?" Gillam says, the smell forcing a cough from her.

The corpses of men, women, and children line the hall of this once great temple. How must they have felt as they were left here to die? Left like vermin, as if their lives did not matter.

As repulsed as I am with the situation, there is nothing we can do for these people, and I make hastily through the storm of flies towards the back of the temple where I know Jordell's study and library await us. Taking the shallowest of breaths, I try not to ingest the death that surrounds us, but the flies batter my face as I make my way through them.

I scramble for the door handle on the other side of the room, and usher Gillam inside before following, closing the door behind us.

I am shocked to see a man and child sitting on the floor in Jordell's study, reading. The child must be no older than four. Both look dishevelled and malnourished. The man's hair is wild and greying, his eyes empty and full of sorrow as he tries to keep the child busy. I cannot tell if the child is his, but the man instantly moves to shield the girl.

I am relieved to see that there is life in this building, but I am saddened by what horrors these two must have endured over the last moon cycle.

"We mean you no harm, friend. We are here simply to collect some effects," I say quietly. Between Gillam and me, I am the diplomatic one, and I hope my words offer some reassurances to the man who stands before us.

There is a feral wildness embedded within his dirty face. Something about him is familiar and I cannot help but feel that I know the man.

"Killian?" Gillam asks in astonishment.

It jolts my mind. Killian is the innkeeper from one of the inns we used to frequent before all this started. His usual tidy hair is now matted and clumped together with dirt.

The man relaxes, but only a little. I would not be surprised if his mind has descended into madness while holed up in this temple of death, but I am relieved when he speaks to me.

"Do I know you?" he asks.

The two of us lower our hoods to reveal our faces. It takes a short while, but before long, he seems to recognise us.

"Vireo, Gillam? What are you doing here? What do you want?"

"We have come for some effects. We do not wish you any harm," I tell him again. Although Killian seems more at ease, he maintains a defensive position.

He just looks at me.

"What happened here?" I ask, dreading the response.

"Jareb," he says. "His mind has become twisted and cruel. We were here visiting my wife. She had been struggling to breathe due to a a sickness in her chest. Jordell was tending to her here." Killian's eyes well up. "Jordell came rushing into this room. Before long, the guards were here. Codrin was leading them."

I know of Codrin, the elvish brute who shows little emotion other than happiness when he inflicts pain on others. He is a dangerous man, and one that Jordell has proven lucky to escape from. Few do.

"It looked like they were here to take Jordell away. I do not know what he could have done to wrong Jareb. The man is a gift from the heavens. Codrin and the guards would have apprehended him if it were not for the boy that helped him escape. I have never seen someone that age so skilled with a blade."

"What happened after they escaped?" Gillam asks.

Killian's face looks pained as he continues, "Codrin ordered his guards to board up the temple. I heard him saying that the sick would only provide more mouths to feed, and their inability to pay taxes meant they were of no use to the crown. They didn't even have the decency to stop their suffering first. They boarded up the doors and left us all in here to die and rot away. Punishing us for being unable to care for ourselves."

Tears streak Killian's dirty face. His daughter walks over to him and hugs him tightly. I cannot ascertain what colour her hair should be, such is the filth that clings to her. She offers her father the comfort he needs and a purpose to carry on living. The man is broken, but he is alive.

"Here, take this." I raise my satchel and remove the bag of coins inside. "There is a hidden hatch in the cellar. Use it to make your escape. Take from this coin what you need and share the rest with others. From what I saw outside, there are a lot. That coin will not be enough to help everyone, but it should be enough for now."

"May the gods bless you both," says Killian, accepting the coin. He grabs the little girl's hand, and they leave without another word, making their way to safety.

"Now all we need to do is find those seeds and get out of here," I say.

Gillam smiles. "You make it sound so easy." She hesitates, then adds, "that was nice of you."

As we continue our search, I can't help but wonder how anyone could overlook such suffering.

39
VIREO

We gut Jordell's study in its entirety. Drawers lie open, books are scattered. We find nothing.

"The room is empty, Vireo. Has this been a waste of time after all?" Gillam says, slamming a drawer shut in frustration.

I rummage through a box on the shelf. There's something there. "No, it hasn't," I say, pulling it out. Inside, I find bandages, needles, threads, and a small bottle filled with a green paste. "This is exactly what we need for Jordell to patch up that head of yours." I grab everything and stuff it into my satchel.

"We still have the library to search for the seeds," I try to reassure her, but she looks ready to strike me in annoyance.

"It will be daylight soon. We need to leave," she snipes back at me with venom.

"If daylight arrives, we'll hole up here for the day and wait it out. Now let's get into that library and search for these seeds." I exit the room and move across the short corridor to the library that sits on the other side. The buzzing hums deeply from the other side of the door to the main hall – a constant reminder of what awaits us.

Getting inside the library is an easy enough task, and I breathe a sigh of relief when it appears not to have been ransacked by Codrin and his men. I still cannot believe that they have stooped so low as to board up nearly thirty sick people with no food or water. No way of surviving. It is barbaric. I never liked Jareb, but I never could have imagined him committing such atrocities. I may be responsible for Allana, but this is on him, and someone needs to hold him accountable for it.

Knowing that time is of the essence, we rush around the room searching for the seeds that Jordell seemed certain would be here. The lighting in the room is poor, and there is an air of dampness that leaves a green mould clinging to some of the books. Just another sign of the once great temple's disrepair. I skim everything quickly, but I struggle to find anything that would be of use to us. Any hope I had quickly subsides.

"Over here," Gillam calls over from the other side of the room. "Here's what we came for. Jordell, you are a god amongst men." She has a grin as wide as her face, a rare sight indeed.

When I inspect her discovery, my face also lights up and that little spark inside me reignites. Maybe we can pull this off after all. Dozens of small paper envelopes are lined up in an orderly fashion. I pull one out and read the label: *potatoes*. I reach for another, and this one is labelled *carrots*.

It doesn't take me long to fill the satchel. Now we have plenty for us to grow our own vegetables.

Satisfied, I turn to Gillam. "Let's go," I tell her, eager to get out of here. As we make for the exit, both of us pull our hoods up again to shield ourselves from the wave of flies.

We quickly navigate the room of corpses and back through the cellar.

The air outside has never felt as fresh as it does now. I drink in as much of it as I can. We both take a moment to appreciate one of the finer things in life.

This appreciation is short-lived as, in our haste to escape the wretched smell of death, we have not noticed the guard walking the perimeter.

He looks straight at us. "You there! What are you doing?" he calls out.

We exchange worried looks.

"We do not seek any trouble, sir," I profess in innocence, but if I need to take this guard's life, I will.

He makes his way towards us. "What are you doing around here? Keep your hands where I can see them!" He adds when I start to reach into my cloak for my sword.

We raise our hands in tandem. There are two of us and one of him, but we know he could shout for reinforcements. He has a slender build, and looks to be in his mid-twenties. He keeps his pike pointed at us as he approaches. His gaze passes over the trapdoor behind us, then moves to our faces.

I fear my hood does not disguise my face well enough, and this is confirmed when the colour drains from the young man's face. "It's – it's *you*," he says, alarmed.

There is tense, split-second moment where we stare at each other. I barely have time to think.

"GUARDS!" the man calls out, but as quick as he calls out for help, Gillam is upon him. She removes both her blades from the harness on her back. With one hand, she uses her a dagger to hit the guard's pike, redirecting its aim. She plunges the second dagger straight into his chest. He gargles blood before he succumbs to his fate and slumps to the ground, crimson pooling around him.

Four guards greet us from the front of the temple, two raising their pikes. One of them removes his sword from his side and grips it in both hands.

Then they see their comrade slaughtered on the ground. "Sound the alarm!" the largest of the guards bellows, and one of them disappears around the corner. It doesn't take long for a bell to ring loudly, disturbing the quiet.

"Drop your weapons," the large guard commands.

I reply by raising my blade.

The three remaining sentries rush forward, bearing down on us. I dodge one of the pikes and grab hold of its shaft, using the guard's own momentum to pull him towards me. I slam my hilt into the side of his head, then quickly step back as the largest guard takes a wild swing at me with his sword. I parry this, and when he swings a second time, I knock his sword away before slicing his throat with my blade. As he drops to the floor, I see Gillam dispatch the third guard. Both her blades are bedded in the guard's chest. Gillam rips them from the man's convulsing body and turns to me.

"That wasn't too bad," she says with a smile, unfazed. "So much for sneaking in and out."

I wipe blood off my sword using one of the fallen guard's tunics. "You know, for someone so good in the shadows, you seem to enjoy the spotlight."

"We need to move, quickly," Gillam says, ignoring me. The bell is still ringing.

Only the gods know if we will make it out of this alive.

40

JAREB

There are many healing qualities that can be produced by all manner of potions. It is just a case of scouring the lands for the right ingredients.
-Zaphire Etsom, Temple of Eltera, 251 KR

Was last night a dream? Have I imagined being visited by Morgana in the dead of night glamoured in the appearance of my dead wife?

I stare at the ceiling above me, a rare smile on my face. The sun is only just rising, but I have finally slept. I do not know for how long, but I feel rested for the first time in ages. I roll onto my right and find that the two chamber-maids are still beside me, innocent as they sleep. Not so innocent when they are awake. Morgana is not here, nor is the image of Allana.

The girl with dark hair and even darker skin stirs. She gives me a flirtatious smile and slides towards me.

"I admire your eagerness, but I am afraid that I need

longer to recover," I tell her. Somehow the two women slept through Morgana's visit – if indeed it was even real.

My stomach growls and I think about the foods that I will enjoy on this fine morning, with a feeling of hunger that I have not experienced since Allana's death.

"Morgana, you are a sorceress," I grumble under my breath. I look forward to setting eyes on her again.

A faint noise rings out in the distance, one that I can't quite put my finger on. Then I recognise it: the bell from the Great Temple – the one I requested to be used only if Vireo or Jordell are spotted.

I have a feeling I know who it's for.

"VIREO!" I shoot out of my bed, grab my tunic, and dart from my chambers, leaving my guests to see to their own needs in my absence. My heart pounds and adrenaline surges through my body. Cold stone sends icy pains into my feet, and I realise I forgot to put on my boots. I grit my teeth and continue to run through the discomfort. There's no time to turn back now.

It doesn't take me long to reach the entrance to the castle. The bell continues to ring out, and I wonder how many guards have already descended upon its location. I hope and pray that Vireo has been captured, and that I will be able to end him myself.

I gulp for air as I hit the main street, my lungs feeling as though they are on fire. A passer-by gets in my way and I shove him to the side.

I sprint through the streets, not caring if the common people witness me in this state – an aging steward, running barefoot across dirty cobblestones like a beggar or a thief. All I care for is revenge against the man who has wronged me and destroyed my life.

Bile makes its way up to the back of my throat, causing

my nostrils to sting whenever I breathe. I home in on the bell that continues to ring, all the while the noise getting louder and louder as I get closer.

I see the top of the Great Temple over the roofs of the houses, and I can hear the heavy clanging of steel on steel. A fight is underway. I skid to a stop when I reach the open streets in front of the Great Temple and take in the scene before me.

I count at least five dead guards strewn across the ground like slaughtered cattle, their blood staining their surroundings. Two more lie wounded on the floor, groaning loudly.

Two figures stand back-to-back. One is a blonde woman in a red cloak, carrying blades in either hand.

Then I see *him, and* all my anger spills out. Wearing Allana's torn emerald hood like a trophy, Vireo stands beside the woman, panting heavily from the fight that has ensued. Then, over the blood-soaked streets, our eyes meet.

Dishevelled, ripped clothes, and covered in dirt and mud. I can't help but laugh at how the mighty have fallen, and I look forward to ending his worthless life. Death, however, would be too kind for this vermin.

I realise I have no sword and no active guards in the vicinity. The bell continues to ring out and I know that more of my sentries will be on the way. All I have to do is stall Vireo long enough for more men to arrive. So that we can apprehend him at last – him and his little sidekick.

As if he reads my mind, Vireo re-resheathessheathes his sword. He has an equal look of hatred for me drawn on his face, his expression contorted with rage.

He breaks out into a sprint in my direction. "Jareb!" He roars, charging me down.

"Vireo, don't be a fool!" The red-hooded woman shouts, but her words fall on deaf ears.

I run to meet him, clenching my fists tightly as we approach one another. Our bodies crash and slam down hard against the cobblestone. I feel the air leave my lungs as I find myself winded where I lie. I do not have time to think before Vireo is on top of me, raining punches. I shield my head, and when I sense a gap between his blows, I force Vireo off me. The morning dew causes my knees to slip as I dive on top of him. I return two or three punches, one of which connects with his face. The satisfaction I feel as blood spurts from his mouth is indescribable. Before I have a chance to land another blow, I find myself thrown back to the floor from behind. I curse at my stupidity in forgetting there are two of them and one of me.

"No!" Vireo calls out to his friend.

"Maybe there is honour amongst thieves. I am led to believe you're still taking things that don't belong to you," I goad him. We are both heavily fatigued, slouched in form, but I must not give in.

Lunging, I strike out at his face. He blocks this, but my next punch lands. Vireo knocks me away and thrashes me over the head and my ears ring, as if mimicking the bell that continues to toll noisily above us. I stagger backwards, but Vireo gives me little time to think; he is in my space quickly and grabs hold of the neck of my tunic.

"You are a coward!" he growls at me with utter hatred.

I throw my head forward and connect with Vireo's nose, which explodes with blood. The ringing in my head gets louder. Vireo grins at me, unfazed by his bloodied face. He headbutts me in return, and I feel my bottom lip spatter blood. The two of us fall backwards, losing balance and collapsing onto stone.

Vireo's friend rushes to help him. "Vireo, this is madness. We must leave now! Will you think of others for a change instead of your own selfish needs?"

My vision is blurred. I hear the galloping of horses from behind me and the stern voice of Codrin calling out from afar. My guards are not far away and I'm just moments away from dealing with Vireo once and for all.

Mark my words, he will spend his days in my dungeon for everything he has done to me.

41
VIREO

The taste of iron fills my mouth. My anger has engulfed me in its entirety.

The beast lies on the ground as bloodied and beaten as I am. I barely noticed the blows he landed, such is the numbing rage that pulses through me. I curse loudly as Gillam drags me up from the ground. I am covered in mud from brawling with Jareb like a pig bathing in filth. Blood drips from my face, and a dull throb settles in.

Gillam drags me down the nearest street away from the temple. I struggle mindlessly against her, wanting to finish Jareb. Then I see Codrin arrive with cavalry, and I start to come back to my sense.

Finally realising the gravity of the situation, I turn and run alongside Gillam in the opposite direction. The morning light has broken, meaning our planned escape in the shadows is now impossible. Our best ally – darkness – is gone.

The guards' voices echo around the empty streets as they shout to one another, desperately searching for our whereabouts.

"Split up! You down there, you four with me," comes the emotionless voice of Codrin, a man simply doing what he is told. I wonder whether he is even capable of thinking for himself. A loyal servant to Jareb's tyranny.

I think of what he has done, of the people left to rot away in the Great Temple, and the urge to run towards him overcomes me.

"Will you get a grip of your emotions!" Gillam hisses, "You are going to get us both killed."

She speaks the truth, and as much as I would like to make Codrin pay for what he has done, I am in no position for another fight. His sheer size alone would make it difficult even if I were at full strength.

The guards are flanking Gillam and me. On horseback, it will not be long before they catch up with us. We hide behind a large building to regroup and plan our next steps. I hear even more shouting and hooves clacking against the surrounding streets. They are closing in. An image of my head on a spike flickers through my mind. But no, Jareb will want me to die nice and slow.

I gasp for breath. The fighting and the running have taken a toll on me. I must dig deep if we are to somehow make it to the storm drains where our planned exit awaits.

Gillam's eyes move wildly across the terrain as she scouts our options.

"I count at least thirty men," she whispers. "If we head south, there are fewer guards that have headed that way. Even then it is not looking good, the daylight has blown any chance of us escaping."

If only I hadn't been drawn into a fight with Jareb, we would have made enough ground to safely make our escape. My rashness will be our doom. I can only imagine the tortures that Jareb has planned for me. What's worse, my sister-in-arms is also in this situation because of me. They'll torture her, I know they will. I might deserve it, but she doesn't.

Looking up at the sky, I pray for some sort of intervention from any higher beings. There are enough gods out there. Maybe one of them is looking down on us.

Gillam lifts one of her daggers. "Our capture is inevitable, Vireo. But they will not take me alive." She stares into my eyes knowingly, as if reading what horrors are crossing my mind. "The least I can do is take down as many as I can," she says.

I grip the hilt of my sword with sweaty palms. My muscles ache, and I am still struggling to regulate my breathing. "In death, there is honour," I tell her, mimicking the words we used to speak before battle. I ready myself for one last fight. We used to talk over ale about how we thought we'd go. In our imaginations, our deaths never looked like this.

Gillam forces a smile. "I always knew you were a fool." Then she prepares to jump out at the guards that are about to ride past our position.

There is a noise behind me, and I am pulled backwards against my will by the scuff of my hood. Ahead of me, I see a heavily damaged doorway. Within a moment, Gillam stands in the arch. She pulls the door shut and suddenly the two of us are shielded from sight.

Spinning round, I recognise the surroundings. Tables and chairs are scattered across the room with no order. Empty glasses and broken bottles litter the surrounding floor, the broken glass crunching under my feet. On the far side, I see the bar where Lek, Gillam, and I had frequented on many occasions.

Between us and the bar stands Killian.

"Keep quiet," he whispers, pressing a finger to his lips. "Kalia is asleep upstairs. This way." He leads us through the ransacked tavern, ushering us into a room at the back of the inn. There is an old set of table and chairs, as well as a crackling fire in a small hearth. An animal skin that I don't recognize lies in front of the fire, tangled with bedding. I position myself by the flames, holding out my hands for warmth. It has been a long night.

"They pillaged this place as soon as they realised I wasn't around," Killian explains. "They have taken pretty much anything of worth. At least Kalia has her bed still. She will sleep well today." He breaks off the leg of a chair and throws it into the small fire. "I don't blame them," he continues. "Everyone is desperate and doing what they need to survive. Thanks to you, I have some coin to share with others and pay the taxes Jareb demands." He stares into the flames, an emptiness in his eyes. "My days as an innkeeper are done. No one has the coin for luxuries such as wine and spirits. It's all gone, anyway. I can only hope it has brought comfort to those that felt it necessary to take."

I am amazed at Killian's restraint. If this had happened to me, I would have been furious and made people give back what they had taken from me. He shows a level of understanding that I've always struggled to achieve.

"That coin will help for now, but it will not last forever," I tell him. "If you need to keep that coin for yourself, I would not blame you. You and your daughter face a hardship."

Gillam peers through the broken window, watching for the guards that roam the streets in search of us.

"My hardship does not differ from what the others face. It would not sit well with me to keep all the coin. I will only take what I need for us to get by for now, and pay what I owe in taxes. The rest I will give to those without a roof over their heads or blankets to keep warm at night."

His selflessness shames me. As I watch the fire dancing in the hearth, I reflect on my actions in the past, barely recognising the pompous collector that took money from the poor.

"It is only a matter of time before the guards start kicking down doors," Gillam says. "We need to find a way to the eastern gate and back to the forest."

"The Forest of Opiya?" Killian asks, confused.

"It is there where we have made base. It's the only place Jareb and his guards will not chase us," Gillam explains to the innkeeper.

"What about the creatures in there? How on earth are you surviving?" His eyes widen at the thought of us living in such a dangerous place.

"By the grace of the gods," I answer. I wonder myself how we have not been picked off by the creatures that roam the darkness of the forest. Creatures we were all told of as babes to warn us off from ever entering its depths.

"I can get you to the eastern gate." Killian stands up tall and moves towards the door. "There is a tunnel below this building, a way of connecting all the inns together for emergencies."

Killian has now returned the kindness we showed him in abundance. I feel the coin is not enough to show the gratitude I feel, and for a moment, I cannot find the words.

I clear my throat, gathering myself. "Can we use this passage to get in and out of the city?" I ask, spotting an opportunity for future access.

"My friend, you can use this tunnel however you need."

42

JAREB

I launch a vase into the wall, smashing it to pieces. The flowers that were inside lie strewn across the floor, and I kick one of the blossoms as I storm towards the table that is laden with food and drink. My head throbs, my body is sore, and I feel nothing but anger. My feet are mangled. Blood and mud mix to form an unhealthy crust around them.

"How were they able to escape?!" I bellow. Vireo was injured. I had beaten his face until he was a bloodied mess. He was in no state to get away from us.

"My men are still out searching for him," says Codrin, who follows behind me, his deep voice echoing in the empty hall.

"*Your* men?" I spin to face him, aware that my clothes are caked in dirt. "You may command them, but those men report to me, Codrin." I am sick of men claiming what is mine for their own.

He nods. "Yes sire. Apologies. They cannot have gotten far. We should be able to head them off before they make it back to the dark forest." Codrin stands tall, far taller than

177

me. If he wished, he could crush me with his power. Luckily the man is loyal, obedient as a dog, someone I am glad to have on my side.

"Should? They have already escaped. They are like rats." Spit leaves my mouth as I curse their existence. "What were they doing at the Great Temple? Why were they there?" It must have something to do with Jordell. It cannot be a coincidence that he was seen entering the forest and now we find Vireo leaving Jordell's temple. No doubt Jordell sent them on some errand to help with the magic that I need to end this war.

At the table, I reach for the jewel encrusted chalice and take a sip of water, wincing as it presses against my bloodied lip.

Codrin has summoned some maids to tend to me, two of which scurry into the room with a bowl of water and some rags. They mop the matted blood and dirt from my face as I sit stewing at my guards' incompetence.

"Increase the reward! One thousand coins for Vireo and five hundred for each of the men and women that follow him. Add Jordell to that bounty as well. He needs to be brought in alive."

"Yes, sire." Codrin bows and exits the hall.

The maids continue to mop my face, but I feel flustered by their presence and shoo them away. I recognise the short-haired one as one of the women who shared my bed last night.

"Run me a bath," I command. The two of them exit as quickly as they entered, neither uttering a word to me.

As the maids leave, Morgana enters the hall, wearing a tight-fitting black gown. She saunters towards me slowly, showing far more composure than I am.

"Tell me, seer, did you see this?" I feel a flicker of guilt for the venom in my voice.

"My lord," she says, bowing. "Perhaps I have not explained my gifts well enough to you. I cannot control what I see, or when I see it." She is reserved in her response, far more than I deserve for the way I have just spoken to her. "I must say, I did not expect to see you in this state on this morning," she says as she delicately places her hands in front of her, pursing one hand behind the other.

"I don't mean to snap at you. My frustrations got the better of me," I tell her. I feel I need to apologise. After all, Morgana is the one person who is helping me more than anyone else. I mull over her words. She didn't expect to find me in this state. Does she mean after last night? I still do not know if it truly happened or if it was simply a dream. It felt real, but if I were to speak of it to anyone, they would accuse me of insanity. The king's steward spouting that he had lain with his dead wife! They would have me locked away and declared unfit to govern the kingdom.

"I nearly had him. Vireo entered the city, and I had him in my grasps," I say.

"It looks as if he has taken a good hold of you too, my lord," she purrs. "Vireo will only cause further distraction. If you are angry, you cannot govern with a clear head. Look at where your mind is now compared to when you first awoke."

Perhaps last night was real, after all, but I fear it would be rude to ask.

"My lord, I need more subjects to test my magic on. This is why I come to you this morning." She rests her hand on my arm in an attempt to comfort me. "You have court this morning. You must pass further judgement on those who have committed crimes against the crown. If you can send me someone younger this time, it will benefit us greatly."

"I will see what the court brings us." I stand up to leave. "I need to clean myself. I will see you at court." Then I look at her, hesitating. "Morgana, can ask you something?"

"Of course, my lord. Anything."

"Is there such a spell called a glamour?" I ask nervously, trying not to sound timid.

Morgana picks up a red apple and bites into it before meeting my eyes and smiling.

For a moment I swear it is Allana's eyes that meet my own.

43

VIREO

I do not believe in the king's war. I do not believe in the suffering we have forced on the people of Levanthria. We need to find another way, there must be a way to end the war. One that does not leave our people in poverty.
-Diary entry of Jareb, 260 KR

"You are lucky to be alive," says Jordell as he applies a foul paste over the injuries on my face. He assures me it will prevent any infection taking hold of me, so I force myself to tolerate the stench. Gillam's head has already been cleaned and patched.

The tunnel beneath the inn provided the route that we desperately needed to ensure our escape to safety. It wasn't the easiest to navigate, but following the instructions Killian gave us, we were able to reach the eastern gate and escape through the storm drains.

Thankfully, our horses remained where we left them, undisturbed and peacefully asleep.

"How did it feel to get your hands on him?" Lek grills me, a wild grin on his face.

"Do not encourage him, Lek, he almost got us killed," Gillam scolds, taking a seat at the campfire and pouring herself a drink.

"But I didn't, did I?" I shoot back smugly. At that, Gillam looks like she would love to add to the cuts and bruises that decorate my face.

"It would seem my plan of giving coin to people has already borne fruit," I continue, smiling at the rest of the group – though I avoid the death stare that Gillam reserves for me.

"How do you mean?" Lek sits like a child waiting for a bedtime story from a parent, an eagerness in his face.

"Killian has provided us with a hidden route into Askela, one that Jareb and his guards do not know about. This provides us a safer route to provide coin in exchange for supplies."

"But the last time I went there, no one was willing or able to trade," Laith points out from afar. It is his turn to stand watch, and he stands by the edge of camp. He is clearly tired; large purple bags have formed under his eyes. "It would be madness to head back into Askela after your last visit."

I nod. "But last time, we had not given the people on the streets coin to aid them through their troubles. Killian is a man of his word. He will share the coin with people who need it. I can guarantee that those very people will be more inclined to help us than they were before. If not from the coin, then from the fight that those on the street bore witness to. Jareb is forcing hardship on everyone. This isn't just about taxes. He has a different agenda. Those that are suffering because of him will probably be spreading stories of the beating that I gave him."

Having tended to my wounds, Jordell stirs the contents in the pot over the fire.

"There is more, Jordell. I am afraid it is not good news." As I tell Jordell of our discovery at the Great Temple – of how the sick were trapped inside and left to die – his expression becomes tortured. He cries out in anguish, his eyes streaming with tears that drip down his cheeks and soak into the dark beard forming on his face.

There are no words of comfort that I can offer him. The men, women, and children suffered badly. Now their bodies serve as fodder for the flies.

"We must find a way to bury the dead," Jordell chokes, stifling further tears. He straightens. "I must go back."

"No," I say quickly. That would be a monumental task on its own, not to mention that guards will be on high alert.

Right now, Laith is the only person able to travel in and out of the city with relative safety.

"I must –"

"No, Jordell. Once Laith is rested, we will send him into the city to pass on your request to bury the dead," I interrupt him. It's the only thing I can think of. I can't risk losing Jordell, because we need him to finish transcribing the spell book.

Lek stands tall, casting a large shadow over me. "For now, you all need to rest, and then we can regroup. I will take over watch from Laith. Once he is rested, he can carry the message to Killian. Jordell, do you know what you are doing with the seeds they have fetched?

He sniffles. "Of course I do."

"Then I suggest you get to work. The sooner you sow the seeds, the better." Lek's expression softens. "I understand you're grieving for the fallen, but we must keep to task if we are to survive in this place."

I appreciate Lek taking control of the situation. My mind is weary and the ache in my bones grows stronger as the morning goes on.

We have a plan. But for now, I need sleep.

44
VIREO

t is said that man made an agreement with the gods to stay out of the Forest of Opiya. In return, the creatures that lived deep within the woodlands would not step place in the villages, towns, and cities that surround it. This does not mean that creatures do not wonder outside from time to time, claiming their victims, leaving nothing but a bloody path in their wake as a dark reminder of their ferociousness. It is said, however, that any man, woman, or child setting foot within the forest is likely not to return. This is why no one steps foot in that forest.

-Diary of Gregor Yerald, explorer and monster hunter, 262 KR

Two moon cycles have passed since we planted the seeds from the Great Temple. This has proven to be a master stroke on our part; the enriched soil of the forest is perfect for gardening. This means we have been able to grow vegetables at a faster rate than anticipated. Jordell deduces that this is because of the magic that resides in the forest, which provides a perfect bed for the seeds to grow and for us to sustain our new life here.

Large potatoes, bright orange carrots, vibrant cabbages, and more serve as a small, manageable crop at the edge of our camp boundaries. We take only what we put into the forest. Jordell has explained that we need to maintain balance while we stay here. After all, we are guests here, and we can stay here only as long as the forest allows it.

From Laith's supply runs, we leave offerings for the wolfaires in the form of pork and beef – an unwritten agreement that appears to have formed.

Jordell has placed rocks strategically around our camp, which he claims will offer us protection. A spell that he learned from the book allows him to draw on the magic from the area, rather than using his body as a conduit. We can only assume that this magic offers the protection Jordell intended. We have not laid eyes on any larger creature within this dark forest since the ogre's visit.

Over the course of the past few weeks, the group has taken on a routine of sorts. Laith continues to make sporadic supply runs into the city, where he takes advantage of the alliance we've formed with Killian and his acquaintances. When he's at camp, Laith spars with me, Gillam, or Lek. Occasionally Jordell joins in, insisting that he must be ready to wield a blade when the time comes. We take turns standing watch, never leaving our safety to chance.

Killian managed to rally some of the locals to round up the bodies of their loved ones and conduct proper burials. For Killian, this was important, as his wife was one of the bodies trapped inside by Codrin and the other guards. After a summons to court and extra payment of coin to the crown, provided by us, they eventually released the bodies.

Killian and the others set to work over the next two weeks, burying them, finally allowing their souls to rest. Jordell seems to take comfort from this, but when he sleeps, I hear his muttered words of distress. He still grieves for each and every one of the souls lost in that temple, blaming himself.

Occasionally, we patrol the roads that surround the edge of the forest, hoping for another caravan to rob.

Against all odds, we have learned to survive in this place. Without the magical properties of the forest soil that has permitted us to cultivate vegetables, we might have perished long ago.

Today, it is a mild morning, and sunlight filters through the canopy above. The weather is kind – a perfect day for caravans to be on the road.

"Are you ready?" I ask the others, readying my sword for the task at hand.

"Must you look so joyous, Vireo?" Gillam responds with a sigh.

"Ignore her. Gillam is just afraid to travel through the forest," says Lek, clipping his great axe to his back. He laughs. "I, on the other hand, will do what I must to obtain the wine we desperately need."

"And coin for the people," Jordell corrects sternly. "You should take Laith with you, too. I will be fine here."

Laith's face ignites with joy. He has been asking weeks to join us on a caravan ambush, but I haven't wanted to risk a bounty being put on his head, too.

Although reluctant to agree, last time we raided a nearby caravan we were forced to leave supplies behind because there was too much for us to carry.

"If you must," I say, surrendering, "but you'll need to take extra care to keep your face covered."

Laith's grin widens at the news and he runs to fetch his

sword straight away. I can't help but smile at his enthusiasm.

"I want you only to observe from the trees," I add. "You stay hidden until I say otherwise. Understood?"

Laith lets out a huge sigh but agrees nonetheless.

"Are you sure you will be ok, Jordell?" I ask, turning to the alchemist.

"My protections spell is active and, believe it or not, I can defend myself. I find your words quite offensive," Jordell says, but he smiles.

I pull up Allana's hood once more, her scent still present but fading slowly. It gives me hope and purpose.

Today is going to be a good day.

45

JAREB

There has been no sign of Vireo within the streets of Askela since the day I had him in my grasp. But there have been multiple reports of caravans being hit outside of the enchanted forest.

They say that the man who leads these ambushes wears a green hood – and even worse, that he is somehow getting the coin he steals into the hands of the people. They act like Vireo is some sort of martyr.

As I sit in my study, writing in my journal, I hear a faint knock at the door.

"Come in," I command. It is Morgana. Her company is a welcome distraction from the stress of running this kingdom.

She walks in seductively, her night gown barely covering her. She is a beautiful woman, and as always, her presence makes my heart race. People see her entering my chamber at night, and there are whispers in the halls of our time together, but I don't care.

The time I spend with her in my chamber is wild and passionate, almost animalistic. I find myself unable to control my urges around her. I wonder how people would react if they were to know I have not once lain with her in her normal form. The nights she keeps me company in my chamber, she does so in Allana's form, making herself look, feel, and smell the same as my deceased wife.

But after, she behaves like a goddess. I find myself entranced just by her presence, even finding my eyes stuck on her when addressing the court, but only ever touching her when she takes on Allana's appearance. She even seems to enjoy it herself.

"My lord." She bends over and leans onto the table, looking at me through Allana's eyes.

"I have court to attend," I tell her. "I cannot be late. People will question my ability to govern."

"I understand, my lord. It's just, I like the way you look at me when I wear her eyes."

Morgana's company has kept me from losing my mind, and I have had no further thoughts of leaping over that balcony since the first night she visited me in my chamber.

"What do you write in that journal?" She says. To my surprise, she attempts to take hold of it, but I grasp her wrist, stopping her.

"My deepest, darkest thoughts. These are for me only," I tell her sternly.

She bows her head. "My lord." She removes her hand delicately and seems frustrated at being told no to something. It is rare I am forced to take this stance with her.

Her unhappiness at my actions is apparent. "I must take my leave, my lord. I have training to conduct with our mages." We now have nine mages that have taken to her teachings, and she claims to be growing stronger and learning how to channel the life forces of others through her magic.

"How long until they are ready for battle? It has been three full moon cycles." I grow frustrated with waiting, but I understand the complexities of what Morgana aims to teach. I want only for the prolonged war to end and for the king to return so I can take my leave of this place.

"Soon," she says. I trust her; she tells me only the truth and has become one of my most trusted advisers, second only to Codrin.

As Morgana makes for the door, she removes her gown, letting it trail behind her onto the floor. She exits in her natural, naked form, letting me feast my eyes before closing the door.

I know she teases me, and I contemplate following her back into my bedchamber and having my way with her before she leaves. I resist, because I am excited by the plan that is set in motion for today. One which I hope will give me the upper hand in my plans for revenge against Vireo. Maybe once I have had my vengeance, I will finally be able to let Allana go.

First, I needed to get myself ready for court. Today, I find out if my trap worked.

One that will enable me to drag that vermin Vireo straight to the dungeons.

46
VIREO

It is not only the Forest of Opiya where the gods display their twisted power. There are many other places around the world where they play out their wicked games.
-Kaya Niper, former priestess of the Temple of Eltera, 221 KR

I lead the group to the edge of the forest, until we come upon our usual raiding spot. Gillam remains hidden on our travels in the dense trees in case we find ourselves ambushed, whether by man or beast.

Lek stands by my side with his axe in hand. It hasn't been difficult for the three of us to best the paid guards we have encountered on our raids. After all, we are battle-hardened soldiers, not glorified sentries. Time and time again, Lek and Gillam have proven their worth and loyalty. I wish for nothing more than to pay them kindly for their faith and bravery.

Laith follows behind, clearing our tracks. Lek smiles as I glance back at the boy. When Lek instructed Laith to clear our tracks, he meant on the way back. Neither of us want to embarrass the boy, so we let him carry on. I can see the pleasure in Lek's eyes, and it makes me laugh to myself. His own father used to make us do similar things when we were young, and it built us up stronger. It is only fair that we impart the same lessons on our charge.

I have become used to his presence in the group. Laith has earned his place with us ten times over, but whether I can trust him fully remains to be seen. After all, we did not meet under the best circumstances. For all I know, he is simply biding his time to have his revenge on me.

"The road is just up ahead. There is a large boulder embedded in the ground. This is what you must use for cover, and I only want you to come out when we have finished our task," I tell Laith, pointing.

"Do you hear that?" Gillam's voice travels through the trees, but her whereabouts are unknown to any of us.

The sound of wheels rolling through the rough terrain can be heard coming from just beyond the bend in the road.

I take position behind a large tree that can hide my presence from our victims.

"I wonder which lord it is today?" Lek says, grinning. His hair and beard are wild enough now only to display his beady eyes and the top part of his cheeks. The man resembles a beast more than ever. If I didn't know him so well, I'd be intimidated by him myself. He has taken to collecting the family crests of the traveling noblemen – badges of a newfound honour amongst thieves.

Getting ourselves into position, I wait with bated anticipation as the horses and carts draw near.

"We have to times this well, gents," Lek says, projecting his voice louder than I feel comfortable with. The last thing I want is for him to give away our position. "It's not always this soon that people travel past, Laith. Sometimes we have to wait for hours," he tells the boy, who is crouching behind the boulder as instructed. "Maybe you're good luck," he adds. Lek appears in dominant spirits, even by his standards. Hopefully, his motivation and positivity will handsomely reward us on this fine day.

The first cart comes into view, pulled by two horses. There is one person steering the cart, with a lightly armoured guard perched next to her. It is followed by two large, sealed carriages, a large blanket thrown over the tops of them to protect the contents. A fourth cart which has seen better days trails behind, along with one driver and another guard.

Two guards and two drivers at the rear, as well as one driver for each of the large carriages. We should be able to overpower them, but I can't help but feel uneasy. Something seems off. Surely there would be more than two guards for such a large caravan?

I bury all thoughts of paranoia, not wanting to be distracted.

I pull Allana's hood over my head to cover my face, an action that has become more habit than practical. Once we stop the carts, they all know who we are. There are posters all over the kingdom bearing our faces offering ridiculous rewards for our heads.

Taking a deep breath, I remove my sword from my side and step out in front of the carts as they approach.

"Gentlemen," I call out, trying to sound as loud and confident as possible. My approach is purposefully arrogant.

The driver of the first cart yanks on the reins and comes to an abrupt stop, the horses neighing disapprovingly at their heads being forcibly pulled backwards.

"And ladies," I add, nodding my head cockily to the

female driver. The other carriages follow suit, barely stopping in time to avoid crashing into each other. The woman seems nervous, not used to facing such dangers on the long road. I find this strange given the route they have taken. Surely they have heard the rumours of our looting here. The guard sits with his hand on his sword, but it is not drawn.

"Usually this is the part where you defend yourselves," I drawl. The guard doesn't move, however, which is strange.

"What is it you want?" the guard stammers. He is a young lad, far too young to be left at the front of a caravan by himself.

"Isn't it obvious?" I tease, "We are here to rob you. Hand over the contents of those carriages and we will be on our way. No one needs to get hurt today."

The guard looks around for the others, trying to figure out how many of us are here.

Nervous anticipation hangs in the air. The longer it lasts, the more uncomfortable I feel. The guard looks too young and inexperienced to be this calm and collected, especially given how much the driver is now visibly trembling. There is something about the situation I don't trust. I see the guard's eyes drift from my location to the boulder on my right and then to the cart.

During each of our previous robberies, there has been some lord demanding to know why the carts have stopped. Today this has not happened.

I stand in silence contemplating my next steps when I hear a cough. I am sure that it comes from the large carriage, which is covered by a large blanket.

Then it hits me.

"It's a trap!" I yell. "Get back to the forest!" As my words leave my mouth, the blankets of the two carts are thrown aside, revealing scores of guards, far more than I can count while on the move. The young guard at the front jumps down and lunges for me with his sword. I parry and strike him in the face with my free hand before hitting him again with the hilt of my sword, knocking him down. Three guards move towards me, the rest rushing Lek, who has made his presence known. Gillam leaves the cover of the trees to fight by his side. To my frustration, the boy has also failed to adhere to my calls to retreat, and he runs into the affray. At this rate, we will all be dead within minutes.

But I am not going to give Jareb the satisfaction of going down without a fight.

47

VIREO

The three guards in front rush me, a tactic I don't expect. Each of them take swipes at me from different angles. I parry away the first two before needing to jump backwards to dodge the third. Laith comes to my aid and swings at one of the guards with his sword, forcing him to divert his attention.

Two against one, now. The guards continue to hack at me, and I knock their blades away over and over. Then a window of opportunity arises and I feign sideways, then slam my sword downwards, catching one of the men by surprise. It costs him his life. I pull my blade from his flesh before quickly striking the second soldier down. Their blood splatters across me, spraying the horses.

Laith is holding his own against his opponent as the two of them trade blows. In front of the second carriage, Lek has charged into the row of guards like a bull. Bodies lie everywhere. With Lek's strength and Gillam's speed, they easily dispatch our assailants.

Laith maintains a defensive stance, and it is costing

him; I can see that his opponent is gaining the upper hand. For some reason, the boy is hesitant to attack.

He has never killed. The thought jumps into my head suddenly. An image of his innocent, eager smile flashes across my mind, and I realise that taking a life is burden I do not wish him to carry – not yet. I step forward and wrap my arm around the guard's throat from behind before pressing my sword into his back. He slumps into my arm, and I let him drop to the ground. His blood marks the boy's defiant face.

"You struck him from behind," he chides me. "There is no honour in that."

"You would have tasted the steel of that man's sword if you carried on holding back much longer," Lek barks, hacking down another soldier with his battle axe. "Vireo offers you a kindness!" The four of us regroup to stand side by side. Then there is movement from beyond the caravan and more guards descend on us. In the midst of the chaos, a group of robed men reveal themselves.

Gillam points at one of the robed men with her blade. "I recognise that man."

She's right – there is a familiarity about him that I can't quite place.

"As do I," Lek growls "He is the mage we took the spell book from!"

In that moment, the mage's hands glow, and my thoughts are catapulted backwards to our encounter in the ramshackle house as I recall the power he possessed.

"Get to cover!" I call out.

He fires a blast of energy at us that I barely dodge in time. The other mages begin to fire multiple blasts towards us. I make for the boulder, and Gillam darts for the trees.

Lek, on the other hand, has other ideas. He charges towards them with his axe raised.

"Go!" he commands us as he takes a blast of energy to his chest. The connection jars his shoulder, but he stays the course. "Retreat to the camp!" He yells as he is hit by a second bolt of energy. He roars like a bear when he reaches the cart, and he crashes into the side of it, knocking the mages over.

"Brother, don't do this!" I call out to him, but I know I don't have long.

"I said GO!" He grabs hold of the underside of the cart and tips it up, distracting the mages. The guards arrive and Lek begins to bat them away like flies, but they soon swarm him. There are too many for us to fight off.

I look for Laith to make sure he has made his getaway, but he is curled up on the ground, crippled in pain. He must have been hit by one of the energy blasts from the mage as he made his escape. I run towards him, but I am met by a tremendous force which smashes me into a tree a few metres away. It takes everything I have to prevent myself from slipping into unconsciousness. I gasp for air, winded by the impact. Further blasts of energy hit the surrounding ground, spraying dirt. I can barely make out Lek through the dust, but judging by the guards bouncing off him, he is still putting up a good fight.

Raw energy shreds the trees beside me. If it hits me, it will strip my skin right off.

I press forward to assist Laith who is writhing in agony. He points towards the trees behind me.

"Go!" he musters the word before collapsing and losing consciousness.

"No!" My voice is hoarse and broken. I feel anguish at not being able to help, but there is nothing I can do as magical blasts devastate my surroundings. I see the guards finally overpower Lek. Another magical energy bolt slams into my shoulder and the pain is unbearable. It knocks me off my feet, flinging me into the cover of the trees. I have no choice but to retreat to camp. I only pray they do not follow, that Laith and Lek are still alive.

I can only hope the gods are listening.

48
JAREB

My concentration wavers. Morgana is normally at my side as I pass judgement, letting me know who it is she would prefer to test her spells on, but today, she is not present. I can't help but feel that Morgana is frustrated with me for stopping her from reading my journal, and that is the reason she is not here.

There are few people left to pass judgement on and I turn to see if there is any news on the ambush I have set in motion with Codrin. I have been waiting for a while, but I wait in good faith. Although Vireo and his men have proven their skill against my guards on multiple occasions, I feel confident that they will not be able to stand against the mages. As the day draws on, I grow impatient for news.

"Tralor Forlung, charged with theft." As Codrin is out on duty, another one of the guards reads out the names of the prisoners and the charges they face in his stead.

An old man stands in front of me, his face long and drawn. His clothes are tattered and torn, and I see why he must be desperate enough to steal. Still, the law is the law.

"Taking things that do not belong to you is something

that this court will not tolerate," I say. I think about the punishment, and because of his age, I can't see Morgana having much use for him. "One lashing and then send him on his way," I rule, feeling that any more would likely be the end of him. The man wails at the relatively soft justice and is dragged over to the post where he will be fastened to receive the consequences of his crime.

As the guard awaits for my signal to inflict the lashing, the sound of carts greets me from behind. The carriages I sent out for the ambush manoeuvre into the courtyard, Codrin amongst them.

When the carriages stop, Codrin jumps down and stands before me, bringing his clenched fist up to his chest. "Sire." He starts, his monotone voice showing no emotion. "We have two prisoners to pass judgement on."

My heart skips and I stand, craning my neck. "Is Vireo amongst them?" I exclaim, like a child receiving a gift.

"I am sorry, sire. Vireo escaped us once again."

My anger surges. How is it he keeps evading capture? "He is proving quite the snake," I hiss at Codrin, unable to hide my disappointment at his failure.

"We do, however, have his second in command and an unknown younger prisoner." Codrin nods to the guards who opens the back of one of the carts. Two guards are not enough to pull the prisoner forward, and Codrin moves to assist them. Grabbing hold of a rope, he tugs it towards him and Lek stumbles out of the cart.

"Coward," the big man says, his spit connecting with Codrin's face.

In a rare display of emotion, Codrin's expression contorts with rage and he strikes the newcomer in the face. The sound of Codrin's armoured fist against flesh echoes throughout the courtyard and Lek goes limp, supported by two large guards. The elf gestures, and the other prisoner steps out of the cart. Codrin drags the boy to where I sit so that I can pass judgement.

I have Vireo's strongest man standing before me, battered and broken. Parts of his skin look charred under his burnt tunic, and there are holes in his chainmail where I presume he was blasted with magic. It is a glimpse of what is to befall our enemies when I send the mages to aid the king.

Codrin picks up a bucket beside me and launches water into Lek's face to bring him around. His thick beard and hair absorb the water, and he comes to.

"Lek Greatburn," I call out for everyone to hear. "I charge you with theft from the crown, as well as assisting with the murder of Lady Allana. How do you plead?" I need to make an example of this creature in front of everyone. He will pay for helping Vireo.

Lek's eyes widen. He looks wild with anger, and he does not respond to my question. I feel my nostrils flare with rage. "How dare you show such insolence in these courts. Speak!"

"We do not know this one's name, he refuses to tell us," Codrin announces, referring to the adolescent who kneels next to Lek.

"Well, aren't you brave?" I goad him. He looks easy enough to break. Between the two of them, I have exactly what I need to lure Vireo out. To force him to join me in this court and face the punishment for his crimes.

"It takes a brave man to strike a man while his hands are tied," the adolescent speaks out of turn. Under normal circumstances, I would be impressed. But in front of all the guards and the people who have come to see the court proceedings, I cannot accept it.

"Know your place," I scold as I walk towards him. He glares at me, unflinching. This one *is* brave. Never mind that. It will make it all the more fun to break him. I grab the scruff of his neck and strike him multiple times. He simply stares back at me, refusing to bite.

"Keep firm, boy," Lek attempts to reassure him. I sense he shares an affection for him, like what you would see between an uncle and a nephew.

"Boy? Is that your name?" I wonder if Vireo shares a similar affection for the boy. If so, I sense a perfect opportunity. "Five lashes for the boy!" I demand.

"No!" Lek calls out. "He is young! Five lashes will remove his skin from his bone."

"That is what I am hoping for," I say, grinning just out of Lek's reach, should he decide to lunge for me. "After his lashes, hang him in the stocks for all to see." I want to make sure no one else is tempted to follow the path these two have chosen to walk. "As you said, Lek, he is young, which is why I have shown him mercy."

"You call this mercy!" He screams at me. I dread to think what would happen if he got his hands on me.

"Ten lashes for the brute," I say, smiling.

There are gasps of shock from the crowd. Five lashings would be enough to finish off a healthy adult man, and I have demanded double for Lek. Given his size, I assume he will be able to take the punishment.

"Give the boy his punishment first," I demand.

Codrin drags the boy to the whipping post. He doesn't put up much of a fight as his arms are wrapped around the post and bound. He may be brave – or stupid – but it will not be long until his screams ring true.

Lek struggles. One of my guards kicks him in the back of the knee before gagging him, forcing him into quietness.

The court grows restless. It is rare that someone so young receives lashes for their crimes, but I am determined to set an example. Maybe his pain will draw out the man I so desperately seek.

"Let the boy go," someone in the crowd shouts.

Another calls, "Yeah, let him go!"

"He's just a boy!"

"SILENCE!" I shout. A few boos start ringing from the crowd towards me like we are in a jester's court. "This boy has committed crimes against the crown, against you all."

"He has not committed crimes against us. He helps those in need!" A voice calls from afar.

I do not know what help the man speaks of, but if I were to show a change of heart now, it would be a sign of weakness, and I cannot have that. Not in front of all these people.

Codrin, having finished binding the boy's hands, moves behind him and rips the clothes from his back, exposing his fresh, untouched skin.

"Stop."

"Don't do this."

"MONSTERS!"

The shouting gets louder and more aggressive. The boy stands tall, refusing to cower.

The boy is brave indeed.

Codrin stands about ten feet away. He waves the whip around in the air as if he is putting on a show. He is getting used to the feel of the whip, waiting for the perfect moment to strike. There is no one in this kingdom as proficient with a whip as Codrin, and I look on as he makes the first crack.

The sound of leather against skin draws gasps of horror from the crowd. The boy does not move or even make a noise. In fact, he does not appear to have flinched at all.

Codrin jerks the whip back, and without giving the boy a chance to recover, he lashes him a second time.

The crowd groans, and the boy recoils ever so slightly with the impact. Blood spits from his back, trickling to the ground. I can only imagine how tightly he grits his teeth to prevent from shouting out.

Codrin waves the whip around again, getting as much momentum as he can before he unleashes the third ferocious strike, tearing skin from the boy's back.

The boy's legs buckle, and I feel he is about to crumple, but he straightens his legs, again not showing any signs of pain.

"He's had enough."

"Let him go!"

"This is savage!"

"This is cruel!"

The pleas to stop ring out like an unwanted morning bell. This is where the lashings would normally stop, where many full-grown men have lain down broken from the punishment. Yet here stands someone far younger, far stronger than them, unwilling to break.

Codrin cracks the whip a fourth time, and this time the boy cannot keep his screams within – but the screams turn into a mighty roar.

Then the roar turns into laughter. He must be in agony, but he is not showing any signs of it.

The crowd seems galvanised, and the people begin cheering and clapping. They appear to be cheering on the boy, encouraging him.

"Keep going!"

"Only one more!"

"So brave."

"Show them you can't be broken."

They stir themselves into a frenzy. This winds Codrin up, who waves the whip around before unleashing it for the last time. The force is incredible as it bears into the boy's back, breaking his skin further, his back now completely crimson.

His roar this time turns to screams of pain and turmoil. His voice breaks as he screams louder than I thought possible.

The crowd falls silent. They have only motivated Codrin to remove more flesh than he would have at this stage.

They are to blame for that one. They are to blame for the boy's suffering. Half the crowd has turned its back, and some have begun to leave, not happy with the horrors of today's punishment.

The boy collapses against the post. I can hear his cries of pain from where I sit, and it brings a crooked smile to my face.

"Put him in the stocks, and send a messenger to the dark forest. To Vireo. We are not done yet."

49
VIREO

The camp feels empty. *I* feel empty. Lek and the boy are gone, and it is my fault. I cannot imagine what fate awaits them in Askela – if indeed they are even still alive.

I dragged myself back into our camp to find Gillam already here, cursing the air as she informed Jordell of what happened. It took the two of them to physically stop me from marching straight to Jareb's castle and confronting him.

Jordell wants me to recover first, and for us to plan our next steps before doing anything rash. He is more level-headed than me.

I sit on the edge of the cart, chewing a mixture of Jordell's herbs to stop the pain I feel in my shoulder, which Jordell has cleaned and bandaged. He assures me it will not take long for the pain to subside, after using his magic to heal the burn on my chest. The parcel in my mouth tastes vile, like fruit that has rotted and decayed.

I feel impatient with sitting around. Surely the others

agree that every minute we spend here is another moment of torture for the others.

"There was nothing else we could have done, Vireo. If we hadn't left, we would have been captured, too," Gillam reasons with me, but it feels like she is trying to convince herself more than me. She tries to hide it, but I know she feels genuine concern for our captured friends.

I think over the confrontation repeatedly, each time challenging myself as to what I could have done differently. Lek made his own fate when he decided to go charging in the way he did. It was Laith lying on the ground in the foetal position that troubles me. If I had paid more attention, I would have seen his plight, would have been able to help him sooner.

"It changes nothing," says Jordell, passing me a drink.

"Pardon?"

"Thinking it over and over again will change nothing. I know that won't stop you from hurting, but torturing yourself will not help them or you."

The healer's words ring true, but it does not stop my mind from racing. I sip the hot drink and try to divert my thoughts to a plan of how to rescue them. I have nothing, no ideas about what to do. They outnumber us in every way.

There's a rustling in the trees near Gillam. She removes her blades quickly and is ready to strike when a familiar face appears through the trees. It is Killian, his grey hair matted with leaves from his journey here. His face is pale and gaunt, his eyes wide with fear. After all, he will have heard the same stories as us about the creatures that live here, and he has just marched through by himself. He looks relieved to see us.

"How on earth did you find us? Are you a madman

making that journey by yourself?" Jordell says, rushing to his side to check him over. "Come, sit here." He directs Killian to a large log by the campfire and passes him a drink, which Killian takes with trembling hands.

"I come out of desperation. Laith told me some time ago how to get here should circumstances need it." He takes a shaky sip before continuing. "He paraded them at the court. He showed no mercy."

I feel my eyes widen and my heart races as I imagine the worst. Has Jareb slaughtered them both like cattle for all to see?

"Laith – he forced him to take five lashes."

"FIVE! What cruelness is this? He is just a boy!" My blood boils, and I wish I knew magic so I could place the vilest of curses on Jareb or his lackey, Codrin.

"It was horrible, Vireo. He took them all. Showed nothing but courage. The crowd cheered for him, praised him for his bravery." Killian stares into the fire wide-eyed, as if trying not to relive it. "Jareb sends a messenger as we speak. I knew I could get here first, using the tunnels. He wants you, Vireo. He wants you to give yourself to him, in exchange for Lek and Laith. I fear it is a trap. I fear he will kill all three of you the first chance he gets."

"What of Lek? What was his punishment?" Gillam presses, concerned for Lek's wellbeing.

"Ten lashes, although I left to bring news to you before he received them." Killian finishes his drink and stands up. "I must leave. If I am seen re-entering, they will know I have seen you. They have closed the gates. No one in and no one out until you are in the dungeons."

I worry how Lek will have fared with so many lashes. I understand the man is enormous, but I cannot see how he will have made it past six or seven before losing consciousness. The blood loss alone is enough to put his life at risk, the chances of infection taking him even higher if he has survived. I feel the colour drain from my face. I have known Lek all my life – we were brothers-in-arms along with Gillam, the three of us always inseparable, and now I fear he will be nothing but food for the crows.

"Thank you, friend, you have given us the faintest of advantages by bringing us this news." I offer my hand, and the two of us shake before he makes for the journey back to the city.

Killian stops on the edge of camp. "I have men and women who will fight," he says. "They are grateful for the coin. They are not happy with what Jareb has done to Laith, given the aid he has provided us these last few moons. Like me, they will fight."

"See what you can do if Jareb is inviting me in. He wants a show. Who am I to resist such an offer? An audience with the man who has done all of this to us, to Askela. I will not stop anyone who wants to take up arms, but I do not expect it. I only wish for them to fight alongside us if they will it." I feel invigorated, a plan slowly forming. "Make haste, Killian, I shall see you at court soon enough."

Killian beats his hand against his chest before disappearing into the forest. I only hope the creatures leave him be, like they have us for so long.

"What do you propose, Vireo? It is clearly a trap. He's using Lek and Laith as bait," says Gillam, looking pale. She does not seem comfortable with any of this.

"We have little choice. This might be our only chance to save them," I tell her.

"That is, if they are indeed still alive." Jordell packs some effects into a satchel.

"What are you doing?" I ask, confused.

"I will not sit around when there is help I can offer to not only you, but to the people."

"What about the spell book?" Gillam asks.

"It is hidden. I have finished what I can for now. The two of us together is what Jareb wants, Vireo. As long as he does not have both, I will not spill the contents of my mind." Jordell walks over to his things and withdraws something I am not expecting. He passes it to me.

It is a bow.

"I crafted it from a broken branch I found in this very forest," he says. Then he reaches back into his things and passes me a quiver filled with arrows. "I whittled these over the last few moons to pass time, often on the nights when I stood watch."

I feel daunted. I have not fired an arrow since taking Allana's life, and I do not know if I have the skill to wield this. "This bow is not like my other," I say. "I have shown not to be the greatest of shot without it."

"Your skill lies not within the bow, but in here." Jordell presses his hand against the centre of my chest. It brings me comfort, and it takes me a moment to regain composure. I gather myself and shake his hand.

"What's the plan then? How are we not going to die today?" Gillam says, a grin making its way across her face. She is always up to the fight, regardless of the odds against us.

"We give Jordell what he wants. I deliver myself at his doorstep, and we end this."

50
VIREO

In the snow-filled northern region of the world, there are stories of a monster hunter, one that cuts down any feral beast he comes across. The only thing more unforgiving than him is the broadsword that he uses to slaughter anything unnatural that walks this world.

-Unknown diary entry, 274 KR

Askela looks enchanting as the sun sets behind the walls of the city. The sky is bright with purple and pink, the clouds making way for the emerging moon. I sit on my steed at the outer edge of the southern gates, taking in this mesmerising view. This could be the last time I see it. I find it fitting that the sky lights up perfectly for me to appreciate its beauty.

My nerves feel calm, which surprises me. I am about to throw myself into the lion's den in order to save Lek and Laith. They would do the same for me. After all, this is how this works – I trust these men more than I will ever trust any other. We may not have numbers on our side, but we have spirit, and spirit cannot be broken so easily.

Raising my hood over my head, I breathe in the faint scent of Allana's perfume. It grows weak as time moves on, but it brings me comfort nonetheless. I kick my heels into the sides of my horse and begin a steady gallop until I reach the castle gates. As I approach, I slow to a trot, making my presence known to the guards who stand above the exterior wall.

"OPEN THE GATES!" one of them shouts down. Within a moment, the large wooden doors swing back and allow me access to the city. It has been too long since I last walked these roads without the need to hide. I am here for all to see, no longer hiding. I am not afraid for my safety, just that of my brothers. Feeling at peace with whatever fate has lined up for me, I begin my ride through the streets, towards Jareb's castle, and my fate.

As I make way, people step outside their run-down homes. They whisper to one another as if awe-struck to see me, talking of me as if I am more than a man. I do not understand why they look at me in this way, as I have done little for these people. Some do not seem so impressed with me; a young man and woman spit as I ride by.

"Curses on you," says the man.

"May you get what you deserve," the woman adds. Both look to have seen better days, their clothes tattered and worn, their faces streaked with dirt.

"Bless you," an older woman calls out. "You stopped my son being placed in the stocks."

There is balance within those that watch me walk to my capture. Some are happy to see me, others not. I hear their voices, their words surrounding me.

"It's not right what they have done to Laith."

"It takes a brave man to offer himself in exchange for others."

More voices call out, and a rare sense of pride comes over me. For once in my life, I feel like I can hold my head up high as I continue my last walk through the city. I've strutted down these streets many times, but it wasn't pride that bolstered me – it was arrogance. Status. An illusion of power. But that is all gone.

Gillam wanted to stay close to me as I made my approach, but I asked her to keep hidden in the shadows, a feat made possible because, for now, all eyes are on me. Gillam and Killian should have reached the inn by now, using the tunnels below my feet. I can only hope they can find a way into the courts in time to assist me. So far, I have heard nothing to indicate they have been spotted, and I can only assume that for now they remain safe and unseen.

The streets are becoming darker as the sun continues to set behind the castle walls. The lamp lighters have already made their rounds and the lamps that line the street illuminate my path. When I pass the Great Temple, a crowd of people swells, murmuring amongst themselves as they cast curious glances my way. Some throw small white roses on the ground as I pass. To my own surprise, I feel my cheeks redden. I do not feel that I deserve such praise and blessings.

I allow my gaze to pass over their dirty faces. They have fallen on ever harder times since I last laid eyes on them. More broken windows, more broken people, all of whom are skinny from malnourishment, empty of any spark. It saddens me greatly to see the hardship that has befallen them. I think back to when I roamed these streets as a free man, collecting debts that people could ill afford. All so that I could maintain the luxuries that I desired. It shames me to think that my actions encouraged and enforced their struggles. Now the people stand here in support of me. My gut clenches with discomfort; was I not still the master manipulator, tricking them to my side by sharing stolen coin? Wasn't this what I wanted? The conflict within me is too great to bear, and I focus on where I am going. Before long, the castle gates are in my sights.

I dismount my horse as I approach the entrance, continuing on foot.

It is my walk of redemption – or damnation. The gods will decide.

51

JAREB

The court is eerily dark. Flickering flames line the perimeter, offering partial light.

Having passed out from pain a short while ago, the nameless boy hangs limply, clasped within the stockade. In the darkness, his blood appears blackened as it weeps from his open wounds. He has shown some admirable determination in the way he has conducted himself today, but what purpose did it serve? He still ended up in the stocks, a helpless and defenceless boy at my mercy.

Morgana stands to my left, dressed in black as if in mourning. Her hat sits tightly against her head, taming all her wild red hair. She is silent, waiting.

"Tell me, have you seen anything of this night?" I ask her, searching for some clarity about what will unfold.

"No, my lord, all I see is the same darkness as you." Her eyes remain fixed on the boy, a sinister smile on her face. I wonder what she has in store for him once all this is done. I can't imagine it being worse than the torture that I have planned for Vireo. I shudder with the excitement of being able to soon impart justice on my sworn enemy.

To the right of the boy, Lek is bound and lies on his side. We shall soon see how this beast of a man stands against an actual bear.

If everything goes my way, these men will be dead by tomorrow, and I can focus on strengthening Morgana's magic. That, and torturing Vireo until he cannot take any more.

My guards and mages are here, ready. Archers perch along the walls, ready to shoot at my command. This is only a last resort. I have faith that between the guards and the mages, they will be able to complete the task at hand.

I am impressed with what Morgana has achieved with the small group of mages in the time that she has had. Her magic is superior, but they have all vouched for an increase in ability since undertaking her teachings. I feel I am in for a feast tonight, to finally watch them in action. Their matching gold-lined, dark cloaks make them look even more impressive. In the shadows of the darkness, they could be mistaken as demons, or harbingers of death. Indeed, this is what I hope they will become.

Vireo is on his way to this very point. I know this because the messenger girl arrived just a short time ago to tell of his presence within the city. It will not be long before I finally come face-to-face with him once more. An eery silence hangs over the court, only interrupted by the odd cough from the guards as the cold of the night sits on their chests.

A shadow emerges. I see the green of his hood first, then he materializes fully out of the darkness. He has come alone, or so he wants us to think. I am not stupid enough to fall for this, but by my estimate, there will be three of them at most, and we outnumber them by many.

As he makes his presence known, I can see from this distance that he is not at full strength. His clothes have seen better days. I can't make out his face under the shadow of the hood, but I notice his shoulder is slightly drooped.

I leave my seat and applaud him sarcastically, all the while walking closer towards him. "Is it bravery or stupidity you have shown in coming here tonight?" I cannot suppress my urge to goad him.

He does not look at me. His eyes are on Lek before shifting to the boy who lies limp in front of him. When he steps into the torchlight, I see a sadness in his eyes.

"Could it be that the great Vireo actually cares for others' needs?" It is a sight I never thought I would see. This is the most selfish man I have ever had the displeasure of meeting. This is the man who only ever acts in his own self-interests, taking from others for his own benefit. All so he could maintain his luxuries, and his cowardice. He is a man who has done everything in his power to avoid going to the frontlines of the king's war. Now he stands prepared to give himself up for the sake of his friends.

Still, he does not answer me.

"You are pathetic!" I growl. I am close enough to him for now.

A breeze forms in the air, blowing his cloak behind him. Vireo appears calm and assured, a sign that his arrogance still remains.

"Tell me, are you ready to face your judgement, Vireo?"

"Will you keep your word and let these men go?" he asks, finally speaking.

"That is what I have proposed, is it not? Your life for theirs. A fair exchange indeed. Although I must admit, the scrawny one may not be of use to anyone for a while." My smile is purposeful; I want him to get angry and lose his head. It is here where he will become rash in his decision-making and I can expose his weakness. "Don't worry, they're alive. Go on, check on them if you don't believe me." I hold my hands out as if offering Vireo a buffet to choose from, all the while grinning to myself.

He checks the boy first, lifting his head up to make eye contact. The adolescent stirs, but he does not seem fully aware of his surroundings. Vireo then makes way towards Lek and kneels beside him.

"Are you ok, my friend?" He places his hand on Lek's shoulder in a feeble attempt to comfort him. He gives him the once-over, then looks back at the boy. A look of confusion crosses his face, and my heart pounds with excitement. Vireo seems to notice that while the boy is covered in blood and in poor shape, Lek is not. The giant is clean, and his clothes are untarnished.

Lek stirs to life, and it brings joy to my face that I simply cannot hide.

"I am fine, brother. No thanks to you." He forcefully pushes Vireo back before standing taller than him, easily snapping the loose shackles that bind him.

"Lek?" Vireo lowers the fabric that covers his face. "What is this?"

"For too long, we have lived in that blasted forest, living off of stolen goods like common folk. You have brought shame to our houses, a shame that I cannot bear any longer."

I wish I could hold on to this moment forever. Vireo looks truly shocked. This is his second in command, his best friend. The ultimate betrayal is playing out like the best of plays, all for my men and me to bear witness to.

"No, this can't be, Lek. Have you lost your mind?" Vireo's face is contorted and distraught.

"I can tell you, my mind is clear." Lek presses his hands into a mound of soft dirt in front of him and reveals his great axe that is hidden underneath. Then, he charges at Vireo, letting out an almighty roar. I never thought I would see the day that the loyal Lek Greatburn would turn against his brother-in-arms.

Lek smashes into Vireo with his shoulder, sending his shocked friend barrel-rolling backwards, a cloud of dirt forming around them. He picks Vireo up by the scruff of his cloak and launches him. More dirt spits up into the air, engulfing the two men.

Through the dust, I can make out Vireo's form lying on the ground. I relish the betrayal he must be feeling right now. Whatever plan he might have concocted with his friends prior to coming here is most certainly unravelling.

"Brother, what are you doing?! Don't do this!" Vireo pleads for Lek to stop, and my smile widens to see him begging like the coward that he is.

"You are no longer my brother." Lek lifts his great axe above his head and brings it crashing down towards Vireo, rumbling the air with his beastly battle cry. Vireo barely rolls out of the way in time.

"Brother, I do not wish to fight you!" Vireo stands with his hands up, panic-stricken.

"Do not call me that!" Lek cries out as he swings his axe wildly at Vireo once more. Vireo ducks, rolling out of its path.

"Fight me!" Lek snarls like a man possessed.

"I will not fight you, brother!"

"I will." A second, slimmer figure appears out of the plume of dust, this one wearing red. I recognise her as

Gillam, the vile woman who often accompanied Vireo and Lek to our meetings in the castle. Always standing in the background, unassuming and silent. She comes forth into the arena, interrupting this most joyous fight.

I move my hand to the hilt of my sword, unsheathe it, and point it in my enemy's direction. This is the moment I have waited for. My body shakes as my adrenaline surges.

"Attack!" I scream as loud as my lungs can muster.

I lead the charge towards my sworn enemy.

52

VIREO

My heart breaks from Lek's betrayal. My brother, my closest friend, has turned his back on us and joined forces with Jareb. Everything we have been through together thrown away like a worn out tunic.

I find myself frozen and unable to fight against him. I gasp for breath as I dodge his axe, my already injured shoulder throbbing in pain. Of all the scenarios I had planned through my head prior to arriving, this was not one of them.

A cloud of dust settles around us, and I quickly survey the area. Guards line the walls above us and at our sides. Jareb stands with his sword outstretched, pointing it in our direction. Behind him stands a woman in a tight black dress. I assume this is the sorceress that Jordell told us about, the one who dabbles in dark magic.

"Attack!" Jareb roars.

Lek lunges towards Gillam, who removes the twin swords from her back to parry the assault.

The guards above us concern me, so I reach for my bow

and fire arrows one after the other. I take down three in quick succession, and their bodies drop. One of them lands on two guards below.

Jareb's men move towards me, and I dispatch two more with my arrows before Jareb reaches me. He takes a wild swing with his blade, which I dodge. I don't have time to grab my sword, so I swing my bow to knock him past me. Jareb keeps his footing and slides to a stop, using the wall to brace himself. His face glowers, his eyes lighting up with nothing but rage, and he charges.

Loud roars of men and women ring out from behind me, enough to startle me. Turning around, I see a swarm of people flooding into the court, some with swords, some with makeshift pikes and planks of wood. Killian leads them with knives in his hands, screaming louder than the others. Relief washes over me, but it's not over yet. The arrival of reinforcements increases our chance of survival, but it doesn't guarantee it.

Gillam and Lek exchange blows as the group swarms around us to meet the guards head-on.

I can no longer see Jareb, and I scan my surroundings again, using my bow to bat away a soldier that swings for me with a pike.

I pull out two arrows and fire them one after the other, each taking out a guard. Using the bow invigorates me, and I continue forward, pushing my way through the chaos towards Laith.

As I reach him, another guard nearly takes my head off with his sword, almost striking the boy at the same time. His sword sticks into the wooden stockade, and Killian grabs him from behind, burying his dagger into the guard's spine. Blood fills the soldier's mouth as he slumps to the ground, lifeless.

Lifting the latch on the stocks, I release Laith, who looks dazed. I hold him up as he slumps against me while the fight continues around us.

"Come on, boy, now is not the time to play dead!" I bark, needing him to respond quicker than he looks like he can. He seems aware of what is going on around us, but he is in pain and drops to his knees. "Now is not the time for this! Get up, boy!" I yell, shaking him. We haven't come this far for him to get us killed now. I won't allow it.

Blasts of blue energy fly past us and I recognise them straight away. "Mages!" I bellow in warning for my brothers- and sisters-in-arms. Not that anyone could be prepared for the chaos unfolding in the courtyard.

The blasts of energy fire into the fold, and bodies are catapulted into the air, smashing into walls, other people, carts, horses. As much power as the mages wield, they do not appear to have much control over it.

Then between the crowd I see the sorceress Morgana entering the battlefield, batting people away from her using only her hands. Flashes of light escape her palms and she takes down multiple fighters with the simple flick of her wrist. She grabs hold of an injured guard who has taken a blade to the gut. I can see her speaking with conviction, but there is too much noise for me to hear the words. Then she points, focusing on a woman who is about to club one of Jareb's men with a plank of wood. To my horror, the woman's stomach bursts open, cascading with blood. Morgana's previously injured guard stands tall once more, undying.

This is the witchcraft that Jordell spoke of. Evil in its truest form.

Morgana is a picture of calmness as she walks through the fight. She sees us and raises her hand to cast a spell. Her hand flashes brightly and I throw myself in front of Laith to shield him from what is coming. I brace myself for impact, but nothing hits us. Looking over my shoulder, I see Jordell. He stands behind me, deflecting the blast. He grasps Laith's shoulder and chants, *"Setum virdo ragarrr."* Laith's eyes spring to life. He climbs to his feet unaided, then reaches for the sword embedded in the stocks, pulling it free.

Jordell switches his focus back to Morgana, and he fires a bolt of energy from his hand at her. "Go!" he shouts. "I will fend off Morgana." Wild-eyed, He removes his sword and charges.

"Shall we?" says Laith, as if he hadn't just been on the verge of death. He shows a level of arrogance only outmatched by me. I force a smile, and the two of us take the fight to Jareb and his men. Killian is holding his own, and Gillam and Lek's fight has taken to the ledges above us. Lek swings his axe at Gillam, who dances around the blows while attempting to strike.

There are bodies forming around us from all sides. I survey the courtyard, looking for Jareb. Mages continue to shower down blasts of energy, but it seems to be tiring them; a few collapse to the ground, unable to sustain their attack. Some fall back and flee inside the castle, too scared to join the fight with steel once their magic is depleted.

Jareb comes into my line of sight. He strikes down a man wielding a shovel, and his eyes meet my own. Codrin joins him, burying his sword into a woman's throat.

"Not the big one?" Laith says. How the boy can show sarcasm is beyond me, and I shake my head at him in disbelief. He responds with a smile. "It's ok, there is a conversation I aim to have with him about the lashes on my back." With a determined look on his face, Laith bears down on the elvish brute.

This is my chance. I charge towards Jareb, sword ready.

"Jareb!"

"Vireo!"

Our swords exchange ferocious blows. My arms tire and the throbbing in my shoulder leaves me weak on my right side – and Jareb knows it. It is a weakness that he aims to exploit as he attacks me from that side, over and over. I falter, and Jareb gashes my arm. I wince, and he takes pleasure in my discomfort.

People are dropping all around me. "Fall back!" I scream, but I do not know if anyone can hear me. At this rate, the battle will end in all our deaths. All I can do is try to get some away to safety.

"Fall back!" Killian's voice rallies.

There is a ruckus to my side, and I see Gillam fall from the ledge above and slam into the ground. "No!" I run towards her, but Jareb bars my path.

"Going somewhere, Vireo?" He gives me a twisted smile, sword raised.

Nearby, Codrin cries out, and his hand comes up to his face. Laith seems to have bested him with his sword.

Killian, who had begun ushering people to safety, now rushes to Gillam's side. She writhes in pain, but at least she is still alive.

Furious, Jareb swings his blade at me again. I parry it, switching my sword to my weaker left hand.

"Is that your best?" It is my turn to goad. Jareb seems to lose his head. He swings wildly at me, his momentum giving him the upper hand. He smashes his face into mine, dazing me. I stagger backwards, tripping over a guard's body, and my sword clangs to the ground.

Jareb stands over me, his face contorted and snarling like he is a feral beast not from this world. He dives, wrapping his hands around my throat. I gasp but I cannot take in air. I lash out, struggling against him, but he continues to apply pressure. I feel frantic as my vision becoming harder to maintain. Reaching for my quiver, I grab hold of one of the last arrows I have. With every ounce of my remaining energy, I drive it into the side of Jareb's head. His eyes widen as his blood drips down onto my face. His grip loosens and he collapses on top of me, but I push the arrow in even further and use this momentum to shove him away.

Getting up from the ground, I take a second to look at his slumped body. Blood pours from where the arrow lies in his skull.

"May the gods show mercy." It is all I can muster as I make my way out of the courtyard and through the castle gates.

The fight is over. Jareb is dead.

53
VĪREO

Many have not made it, but there is still a large group of us. Jareb's forces do not follow us out of the city. Many of us are injured, and Killian pulls Gillam in a bread cart. My entire body is wracked with concern for her wellbeing.

"She will be ok when we reach our camp, Vireo," Jordell attempts to reassure me, but I cannot help but worry.

We arrive at our camp in the forest, only now our numbers have grown beyond measure. I have yet to count how many people have joined us in the relative safety of the forest, but it is far more than I could have ever imagined.

The group cheers loudly at our perceived victory, but I can't help but wonder what it is we have actually won. Jareb may be dead, but we are still reduced to hiding in the trees. We cannot step foot in Askela ever again, having taken the life of the king's cousin and steward.

"I will heal Gillam. In the morning though, I will need to leave camp, Vireo."

I take a deep breath, weary. "Why, Jordell? You are

needed here." I have so many questions whirling through my head.

"There is a great war coming, Vireo, one which involves magic and bigger, unimaginable things," Jordell says.

"How do you know?"

"While battling Morgana. When I made contact with her, we shared a vision." Jordell wears a dark expression of concern. "I fear if I divulge too much, it may change the course of things to come. This is how Morgana manipulates people to her will, but it is not the path I can walk. After all, magic carries an addiction that can lead to corruption of the soul. Her soul is already corrupted. I must save my own."

"Where are you going?"

"South. I cannot tell you where, but I must also request a favour." Jordell is pained by what he is asking. The fact that he is not allowing himself to rest properly before leaving tells me the importance of the situation.

"We will repay you in any way we can."

"I need to take Laith with me. He plays a far bigger part in this than you or I can truly understand. He cannot know this, however. I will protect him. I will teach him what I can, and when the time comes, he will be ready." Jordell busies himself with preparing a potion for the injured, chopping and crushing herbs that I do not recognize.

I have no claim over the boy, but I have grown fond of him. The courage he shows is like no man or woman I have ever met. I am proud to have spent this time with him. "Take the boy if you must, but what training do you speak of? What is it you are preparing for?"

"As I said, I have seen a great battle. Years from now, our army will need someone to lead them."

"And what of us?" I press, hoping that Jordell has seen what fate is bestowed on us.

"You have many mouths to feed now, many people to guide and protect. Just remember to respect the forest you reside in. As long as you do this, my protection spell will keep you all safe." He smiles as he carries a paste over to Gillam. "That, and the wolfaires."

It is an enormous burden to place on me, but it is the least I can do for these people. If not for their help, we would not have been able to escape tonight with our lives.

I stare at Laith, who sits drinking with Killian and the others, celebrating our victory. I smile at how happy he is and cannot help but think that he is destined for greatness.

My father once told me that the gods do their work in strange ways, sometimes sending heroes or messengers to unknowingly do their bidding.

As I watch Laith toasting and laughing with the others, I can't help but ponder what further role he has to play in all this.

As if he were sent from the gods themselves.

54

CODRIN

My magic grows stronger with each experiment I carry out. With each life I take, I feel myself becoming more powerful. These subjects are proving to be most useful. I can only hope the king's steward continues to prove his worth in providing them for me. It is only a matter of time before I can put my plan in motion, only a matter of time before the world will know my fury.

Diary entry, Morgana, 260 KR

Lord Jareb is dead, slain at the hands of that coward, Vireo.

Not all who fought against us got away, and they have been dragged away to the dungeons at Morgana's request. I wanted to kill them all for their treachery, but Morgana was able to bend me to her will with ease. It is as if she hears my thoughts.

No sooner do I think of her, she appears by my side and joins me as I look over the dead.

"Are you ready, Codrin?" she whispers in my ear. She places her hand on my face where that boy slashed me with his blade. My pain stops almost instantly. "I can heal the wound but not the scar that it leaves behind," she says.

My vision in my right eye feels blurred, but at least I still have my eye. "Thank you."

"Someone needs to lead these people," she continues. "Someone who knows no fear, who will continue Jareb's good work." Her words feel almost hypnotic as she purrs in my ear. "I have seen the future, Codrin. Two futures, in fact. Different in paths, different in how they turn out."

I turn to face her, intrigued by her words. Jareb confided in me that the sorceress was a seer, so I have reason to believe what she is saying. However, I do not trust her.

"Go on, what do you see?"

"There is a great war coming, Codrin. A war unlike anything Levanthria has ever seen."

"You mean our fight against the Zarubians?"

She gives me a vague smile. "A war. And a sword embedded in stone."

SIGN UP AND DOWNLOAD THE LEVANTHRIA SERIES
EXCLUSIVE, **A LOCH OF GRACE AND GREED**, FOR FREE

You can get this book **for free** by going to:

www.linktree.com/apbeswick

You may unsubscribe at any time.

ISBN: 978-1-7398218-1-4

Editing by Quill & Bone editing
https://www.quillandbone.com

Published By A.P. Beswick Publications

ALSO BY A.P. BESWICK

The Levanthria Series

A Sea Of Sorrow And Scorn

A Frost Of Fear And Fortitude

A Kingdom Of Courage And Cruelty - Pre Order

A Stone Of Destiny And Despair - Pre-Order

A Loch Of Grace And Greed - Read for free by joining my newsletter.

Dust - Free Short story

The Spirit Beast Series

Arnold Ethon And The Lions Of Tsavo

Arnold Ethon The Eagle And The Jaguar

Arnold Ethon And The War Of The Roses